KINGDOM OF DARKNESS

Hank Maxwell and Brad Tucker came to Biafra to make money, flying as mercenary pilots in the civil war. To them the conflict at ground level was remote, until their Czech fighter is shot down over the mission at Bumaru. Here, Maxwell falls in love with courageous Mary Kerrigan, and when the mission is bombed by those who were once his friends, he begins a perilous journey to evacuate a truckful of sick and wounded children through the war zones.

CHARLES LEADER

KINGDOM OF DARKNESS

Complete and Unabridged

LINFORD
Leicester

First published in Great Britain

First Linford Edition
published 1996

British Library CIP Data

Leader, Charles, *1938*–
  Kingdom of darkness.—Large print ed.—
Linford mystery library
1. English fiction—20th century
2. Large type books
I. Title
823.9'14 [F]

ISBN 0–7089–7979–3

Published by
F. A. Thorpe (Publishing) Ltd.
Anstey, Leicestershire

Set by Words & Graphics Ltd.
Anstey, Leicestershire
Printed and bound in Great Britain by
T. J. Press (Padstow) Ltd., Padstow, Cornwall

This book is printed on acid-free paper

1

MAXWELL saw the armoured column from thirty thousand feet; a green and black metallic snake of trucks, jeeps and Land Rovers descending the twisted road. It was moving at strike speed, dappled by alternating patches of sunlight and jungle shade, sinister as it uncoiled its length where the going became easier on the rutted road. At the end of the road, only one hundred and thirty-five miles away, was Lagos, the Federal capital of Nigeria. Once the bright new goliath of hope on the western flank of an awakening continent, Nigeria was now the bleeding giant of Africa.

The ground troops wore the rising-sun shoulder flashes of the new declared Independent Republic of Biafra. They were mainly Ibo tribesmen from the great forests east of the Niger River, which they had crossed in a two-pronged surprise break-out attack two days before. After five weeks on the defensive the Biafran assault had caught the surrounding Federal forces unaware and Benin City, the capital of the Mid-Western region, had fallen quickly to the rebel advance. The Biafran Air Force, in the shape of two ancient B 26 bombers, had terrorized the Federal army and then dropped bombs in the suburbs of Lagos. The Biafran commanders were quick to exploit Nigerian confusion and shock with a fast, determined push to the west. They saw a golden opportunity to finish the war with one bold, decisive strike at the seat of government.

Brad Tucker stopped chewing for a moment, shifting a caramel toffee to one cheek. "Look at them monkeys go!" His voice was a slow drawl. "They're moving like bare-assed broads in a brothel. It's too bad they ain't gonna make it."

Maxwell glanced over his shoulder,

grinning briefly. His square-jawed, rough-textured face was browned by the sun and rasped by the years. His eyes were blue with the corner creases deeply defined and his teeth gleamed white. Back in Korea they hadn't called him 'Smiling Hank' for nothing and the name had stuck.

"War is an old bitch, Brad." Maxwell shrugged one shoulder as he spoke. "And anyway, those are the bad guys. If they succeed in busting Nigeria down into a mess of tribal states then the same thing can happen all over Africa. Our job is to stop it, that's why we were hired."

Tucker nodded and resumed the rhythmic movement of his jaws. He chewed caramel toffees the way other men smoked cigarettes, claiming it was cheaper and he didn't risk cancer of the lungs. Maxwell turned back to the controls.

The two Americans shared a long, relaxed friendship. Tucker had been Maxwell's crew chief in Korea, and later his partner and co-pilot with Max-Air Freight Services which they had run together with a couple of old Dakotas in Kansas.

Those had been the good times but Maxwell didn't think of them now. He squinted sideways into the sun and saw the second Delfin L 29 cruising parallel to his port wingtip. With slanted wings set well back along the fuselage the Czechoslovak jet had the forging thrust of a predator. The two fighters, both flashing silver fire, were hungry sharks prowling the vast blue ocean of the sky. Below them was the scent of blood.

Maxwell pressed the speech button on his radio.

"Delfin Leader to Delfin Two, there's a rebel convoy beneath your starboard wing. Over."

"Delfin Two to Delfin Leader." The harsh South African accent of Lou Hendrix boomed over the airwave and grated against Maxwell's ear. "I see it, man. Let's get down and show those

4

bloody kaffirs just who is bloody boss around here."

"Delfin Leader to Delfin Two. I'll take out the leaders and block the road. That should make it nice and easy for you. All you have to do is follow me down. Over."

"Delfin Two to Delfin Leader. I'll be right behind you, man!"

Hendrix sounded enthusiastic and Maxwell smiled. He knew exactly what the South African was feeling. It was a long time since he had last shot up a military convoy, in Korea where the landscape had been a pattern of bleak greys, ice and snow, and where the Migs could come screaming out of the sun at any moment with all guns blazing. This was vastly different, with tropical jungle sprawling in warm green waves to every horizon and no threat from bandits in the sky, but the old combat thrill was coming back just the same.

Maxwell knew that Hendrix hadn't flown in anger since World War

Two, so for him the thrill would be even keener. He just hoped that Hendrix hadn't got too rusty over the intervening years.

"Hang on, Brad," he warned briefly as he pushed the stick forward. He banked the plane in a wide, lazy loop that brought them down ten thousand feet. The convoy had disappeared beneath his tail but as he completed his turn it reappeared again ahead and to his right. The long snake of vehicles was moving at the same smart pace, unaware of its danger, and Maxwell opened his throttles to overtake. The Czech fighter responded as surely as the old Supersabre he had piloted in Korea, and for the first time he forgot the strange fact that he was flying an aeroplane which had been manufactured on the wrong side of the iron curtain.

In less than a minute the convoy had again fallen behind and he made his second turn. He had all the time in the world but suddenly his instinct was to do it the old way, to go in for the kill as though seconds were vital and all hell could break loose at any moment. He flung the plane into a tight, screaming turn that lined him up on the road for a head-on attack. Still holding the stick down he watched the road and jungle rushing up to meet him in a brown and green blur, and then the lead vehicles of the convoy leaped into his sights.

He pressed his firing buttons to release batches of wing rockets and then raked the whole length of the convoy with canon fire as he levelled out of the dive. He saw the explosions rip the trucks apart, uprooting patches of jungle and cratering the road. Then he had to haul back on the stick and climb.

When he could look back he saw that the leading jeep had been blasted on to its side after nose-diving into the jungle. At least two of the trucks were blazing furiously and the whole convoy had crashed to a halt. Some of the vehicles had lurched off the road and others had come to grief in the rocket craters or smashed into each other. Men were spilling out of the wrecked trucks and running desperately for cover.

Streaking over the scene and adding to the carnage with all guns and rockets blazing was the second Delfin jet. Maxwell saw another truck explode as a canon shell scored a direct hit on the petrol tank and the fireball blazed bright orange beneath the spreading pall of smoke. A moment later Hendrix was climbing to join him in the clean blue sky, where they could view the results of their work with professional detachment.

"Man, isn't that bloody beautiful?" Hendrix asked.

Maxwell smiled. "Delfin Leader to Delfin Two. We'll go back and make another run for luck. Some of those vehicles could still get mobile."

He was circling as he spoke. His second run followed the same path as the first, letting fly the remainder of his rockets and then hammering the shattered convoy with canon fire. There was no resistance, for the Biafran soldiers who did not sprawl dead or dying in their trucks or across the road had fled into the forest.

Hendrix made his second run with the same careless ease and both planes regained height for a final survey. Every truck was now on fire and the black smoke was spreading thickly to blot out the finer details.

Maxwell stared down and felt the combat thrill fading. He was making the mistake of wondering what it was like to be down there, on the receiving end, and he knew that kind of thinking was fatal, something no combat pilot could afford. He had to remember there was a war on, and a quick defeat for the rebels meant a quick end to the war, and less suffering for the civilian population.

Plus he was being paid two thousand five hundred dollars per month, tax free, straight into a Swiss bank account, and they badly needed the money.

He drew a slow breath and spoke into his radio.

"Delfin Leader to Kano Base. You can tell Lagos they can rest easy tonight. The Big Bad Biafrans won't be coming any closer. We've stopped their advance."

Kano control were delighted. The radio bubbled with congratulations and excited demands for more details. Hendrix obliged with a cheerful description of the chaos below. Maxwell wished he could share their elation and wondered if he was getting old. He glanced back at Tucker sitting silently in the trainee pilot's seat behind him and saw that his friend's full-jowled face was motionless and without expression.

"It isn't always this easy," he said slowly. "Sometimes the flak is a bloody nightmare and the Migs can shoot you up before you even see them. In Korea a lot of the guys never came back."

Tucker nodded wryly. "I know,

Hank. But one minute those monkeys are going hell for leather. The next — splat! I guess I just didn't realize how sudden it happened."

"They hardly knew what hit them," Maxwell agreed. Then he turned back to the controls. He gave Hendrix the order and they headed north for Kano.

For a while they cruised high above the great tropical rain forest. There were vultures and eagles in the air currents below, but nothing that could keep them company at this altitude. The carpet of treetops broke up into a confusion of jungle and bush and then came the majestic, blue-grey sprawl of the Niger, the *river of rivers* which flowed from Timbuctoo on the edge of the Sahara through a thousand miles of mountains, deserts, mudflats, forest, jungles and swamps to its mangrove-choked delta in what was literally the sweating armpit of Africa.

North of the river was more dusty bush, becoming slowly more arid. Maxwell let his imagination play along

11

the river until it was far behind, thinking of gold, slaves and ivory, and bloody battles for jungle kingdoms. His thoughts drifted unchecked and suddenly he was dreaming of the good times again — and Claire.

* * *

He had met and married Claire after his return from Korea. It had been a very successful and happy partnership. Claire was not only lovely to look at and athletic in bed, she also possessed a very sound head for business and two hundred thousand dollars inherited from her father. Together they had set up Max-Air Freight Services. The airline prospered for ten years before Claire fell sick with an incurable stomach cancer. It took her a year to die, and while Maxwell nursed her the airline died with her.

For the next six months Maxwell had wandered aimlessly, first in the States and then in Europe. Tucker had stayed with him out of friendship and they were together in a bar off the *Rue Royale* in Brussels when they finally found a job. They were approached by a young negro who wore a neatly cut maroon suit, a cream shirt with bold red stripes and a dark red tie. The African had introduced himself casually, and with a hint of humour, as Colonel Black.

Two hours later they had been recruited into the Nigerian Air Force, ostensibly to teach young Nigerians how to fly. Two separate sums of 7,500 dollars, representing three months advance pay, had been deposited into new accounts opened in each of their names with the Swiss Bank Corporation in Geneva, and twenty-four hours later they had arrived in Kano.

They piloted a few training flights in Dakotas, but quickly training and operational flights were combined. There was a war on, the Nigerians had argued reasonably, and it couldn't wait until the new Nigerian pilots were fully trained. The two Americans hadn't expected anything different so they didn't complain.

The arrival of the two Czechoslovak Delfin L 29 jets was a surprise, but with his Korean war experience flying Supersabres Maxwell was the natural choice to take over one of the new planes. Tucker could have stayed with the Dakotas but he preferred to fly with Maxwell as navigator and co-pilot.

Their first job with the new fighters was to smash the Biafran column advancing upon Lagos.

* * *

Their second major surprise was waiting on their return to Kano Airfield. There was a ten minute delay before they were given clearance to land and as he brought the Delfin down on to the main runway Maxwell saw five more of the gleaming Czech fighters parked in a neat row to one side, while at the far end of the field half a dozen massive transport planes were unloading cargoes of large wooden crates.

Maxwell shut his throttles and braked, bringing the jet to a stop on a half turn at the head of the runway. He was frowning and his eyes narrowed beneath the rim of his helmet.

"Russian Ilyushins!" Tucker recognized the heavy transports immediately. "What the hell are they doing here?"

Maxwell was watching the crates, a dark suspicion forming swiftly in his mind. The Nigerian labour force, supervised by a thick-set European with heavy, unmistakably slavonic features, had already started to pull one of the long crates apart. They paused to watch the two jets land, but they had got far enough for Maxwell to recognize the fuselage shape with the bubble cockpit and the blunt nose of an old enemy.

"They're freighting in Mig 17s," he said slowly. He made a quick count of the crates. "At least half a dozen."

"Jesus!" Tucker said. "This air war must be hotting up."

15

Maxwell nodded. Delfin Two was now down and crowding his tail so he completed his turn and led the way back up the runway. As he parked he saw that the daily Nigerian Airways flight from Lagos was unloading in front of the main passenger building. Descending the gangway was a familiar figure in a maroon suit. He was conducting two young men who were not Africans and led them quickly into the building ahead of the small knot of remaining passengers.

Maxwell switched off and pushed back the cockpit hood. He climbed out of the aircraft and dropped to the tarmac. Tucker followed him down. Here at ground level the air was hot and dry with a thick taste of dust. The heat made them sweat almost at once and they lost no time in unzipping their flying suits and hauling off their helmets. Maxwell revealed a crudely hacked thatch of straw-yellow hair. He had never wasted time on fancy haircuts. Tucker was beginning to go bald.

Lou Hendrix joined them. The South African looked like one of the old *voortrekkers*, big and solid with blunt features and a scorched red neck. He was in his late fifties and starting to run to fat. He grinned cheerfully.

"Man, you see those new Delfins? I hear they've hired six more pilots from Jo-burg to fly them. These kaffirs know how to start a war, but they need white men to show how to finish them."

"Let's get de-briefed," Maxwell said. "I need a shower."

"And a beer," Hendrix agreed. "No, two beers, at the very least."

They walked quickly into the building, heading for the large side office which served as their operations room. Here a group of Nigerian Air Force officers, all non-flyers, told them what was expected of them and listened to their reports. Usually at least one member of the group would meet them on the tarmac when they returned, but

Maxwell guessed that their return had not been intended to coincide with the arrival of the regular passenger flight. It was a typically African bungle, and no one was prepared to show his face to admit any public responsibility.

They had almost reached the debriefing room when he spotted the maroon suit again, and on a sudden impulse he changed course towards it. Colonel Black had been stopped with his two companions by an African airline official who was obviously asking stupid questions. The scowl on the Colonel's thick-lipped face was one of sharp irritation. His two charges stood by stiffly and silently, their faces without expression. The dark one had the fierce brown eyes and hawk nose of an Arab. The other had fair hair, blue eyes and high cheekbones. Both men were in their mid twenties.

"Hello, Colonel," Maxwell said pleasantly. "Still recruiting?"

The man in the maroon suit turned. He licked his upper lip uncertainly, which was an unconscious sign of embarrassment.

"Mister Maxwell, hello — " He searched for an evasion. "I trust you are enjoying your new work. Are your quarters comfortable?"

"The job's okay. It's good to be flying again. The accommodation's okay too." He turned to the two strangers. "Hank Maxwell, I'm from Kansas. Brad Tucker here is from Nashville. And Lou Hendrix from Pretoria." He smiled easily and waited.

The Arab stared back at him and said nothing, but the blue-eyed boy had been taught to be polite.

"I am Lieutenant Vlado Culik," he said slowly. "I am from Prague. My friend is Major Assab, he is from Cairo."

"You're here to fly the Migs," Maxwell guessed. He looked to the recruiting officer for confirmation.

The man in the maroon suit was angry. He shot a bitter glance which threatened a savage reprimand to the official who had delayed his escape.

"It was written into the contract of sale." The admission was sullen and reluctant. "The Russians will not allow just anyone to fly a Mig. Now, please, we must go. And you must attend to your de-briefing." He gripped the Czech and the Egyptian firmly by their upper arms and hurried them away.

"A commie and a wog," Hendrix said while they were still close enough to hear. "Man, will we be flying with some queer company."

"It figures," Tucker said. "Can you imagine the fuss if a Mig 17 was shot down over Biafra with an American or a South African pilot?"

Hendrix chuckled at the thought.

Maxwell merely nodded as he watched the new arrivals move out of sight. He had accepted the civil war in Nigeria at face value, even to the point of flying a Czechoslovak jet. But he had fought communism and Mig 17s in Korea, and the prospect of flying alongside the old enemy aircraft while the Russians pumped in arms shipments behind him was a disturbing new twist. Maxwell had to believe in what he was fighting for and suddenly he had doubts. The issues at stake in Nigeria were no longer as clear cut as before.

He followed Tucker and Hendrix to the de-briefing room with a deepening frown.

2

THE last thing Captain John Okwela had expected was to be attacked from the air. He was riding in the rear seat of the leading jeep, immediately behind Major Okunnu, the battalion commander, when abruptly the streak of silver hurtled towards them at tree-top height with its wing guns spitting bright flashes of red fire. Their driver swerved the jeep off the road and in the same moment Major Okunnu's head disintegrated in a crimson fountain as the green wall of the forest crashed all around them.

Okwela was thrown clear and lay stunned, his mouth and nostrils were filled with the taste and smell of the decaying mould in which his face was buried, with the smell of fresh sap from the broken leaves and branches, and most of all with the sickly reek of the major's blood. He heard the jets thunder overhead, combined with the crack and thud of explosions and the savage hammering of cannon fire. From the column behind him he heard the crash of vehicles and the screams of men.

He pushed himself to his feet and stumbled back to the road. He was dazed but his mind registered chaos and confusion. The leading truck was a bonfire with the cab shot to pieces and two dead men inside. Shrieks came from the back as though the flames were talking tongues of agony. In all a dozen trucks were on fire and the remainder had either crashed into each other or into the trees. The soldiers were scrambling into the road, some running blindly for cover, others milling helplessly in the open.

"Everybody take cover!" Okwela yelled as loud as he was able. There was smoke and dust in his lungs and his chest hurt. "Get the wounded and the weapons under the trees. Drivers with sound vehicles, try and drive your trucks under cover!"

He ran back along the road, weaving through the shattered trucks and shouting his orders. Some men stared blankly, others obeyed, and some he pushed violently into action. He made a dozen instant decisions and then the jets attacked again. An explosion caused the earth to heave and Okwela was hurled into the bush by the blast. He lay there as though dead, sprawled head downwards on the slope at the roadside while his blood seeped slowly through the long rip in the upper sleeve of his tunic. The red stain soaked its way through to the shoulder where it began to blot out the rising sun insignia that was already soiled with dust and dirt.

In his delirium John Okwela dreamed, the images flittering through his tortured mind in stark patterns of red, crimson and scarlet induced by his pain. He was a boy again, running toward the mission at Bumaru where the cross of God dripped blood into the pink dust. He saw the priest and the nuns waiting on the verandah, unexpectedly evil silhouettes in black and white, for the priest's hair was as white as the cowls worn by the nuns. They were beckoning him home but suddenly he was afraid and he stumbled to a stop. Theirs was a false faith, it had betrayed him and he had rejected it, but he still feared it. He did not dare to go back. He turned and fled across the red landscape and through the fiery bush. The sky and forest burned and the priest and the nuns cried out to him with lost, pain-filled voices in the wilderness.

He had been raised at Bumaru, along with other orphans who had been brought to the mission unwanted from the forest. There he had been taught to read and write, to sing hymns and to pray to a God called Jesus. He had believed in the Christian God because he had a full belly and a clean shirt, and because it was wonderful to believe that Jesus would watch over him and protect him for all his life, and then into the spirit world beyond. John Okwela had been a good mission boy, filled with a wide-eyed faith and complete trust.

He had stayed at Bumaru until he was eighteen years old, in the October of 1960 when the Federation of Nigeria had at last achieved its long-awaited independence from British colonial rule. A glowing, dynamic future was painted for the giant new state, which with its vast bulk and enviable natural resources was proclaimed as the progressive leader of modern Africa. The withdrawal of the British meant a sudden demand for trained Africans to take over as technicians, clerks, civil servants, teachers and doctors, and these had mostly come from the mission-educated Christians of the Ibo and Yoruba tribes of the south. The Catholic Missionary Society which financed Bumaru had sponsored John Okwela to study law at Lagos University, and he had left

Bumaru with the blessings and good wishes of the priest and the nuns ringing in his ears.

He remembered boarding the ancient bus that had taken him on the first part of his journey. He had worn a new suit and carried a new canvas suitcase and his chest had been filled with pride and heartache. Now his chest was filled with pain and fire and the bus had diminished in size. There was no roof and the white core of the sun burned through his closed eyelids. He was the only passenger and the shrunken bus was careering wildly through a red nightmare. He cried out for it to stop but the driver was a fiend of Satan carrying him to hell and his cry was ignored. He struggled and then fell back on a darker wave of pain.

His subconscious mind skimmed over the years when he had been a slave to work and study in Lagos, only focusing again when it reached the face of Victoria Amakiri. There came a vision of Victoria kneeling beside him before the chapel altar at Bumaru. Her wedding dress was scarlet and the face behind her red veil was a grinning death's head with eye sockets filled with blood. Okwela screamed in torment.

After his marriage to Victoria Amakiri, Okwela had moved to the northern city of Kano to join a firm of practising solicitors. There were greater opportunities in the Moslem north, where Islamic schooling had been less concerned with preparing its pupils for modern professions. There were risks, for twice before under British rule the dominant Hausas had reacted violently against the better educated foreigners in their midst, but this was the brave new Nigeria and it was hoped that degenerate tribal passions were a thing of the past. Besides, Okwela and his young bride were both practising Christians, and Jesus would take care of them.

In two years Victoria bore two sons, healthy, gurgling black babies whom they christened Matthew and Mark.

Then, during the political elections of 1965, Nigeria started to fall apart. The political struggles were basically the old tribal battles for supremacy reappearing in a new form. The elections were swamped by a wave of terror, with demonstrations, riots, arson and murder ruling out any hope for the infant principles of democracy. Tribal gangs waged war with axes, knives and poisoned arrows and throughout the country some two thousand people died.

Okwela and his growing family survived untouched, because Jesus was taking care of them.

Then in January of 1966 came the first army mutiny. The charade of the elections had failed to break the political domination of the numerically superior Moslems of the north and so the army moved. An alliance of young majors struck simultaneously at their military and political leaders in Lagos, Ibadan and Kaduna. The Moslem Prime Minister and half a dozen of his senior ministers and generals were swiftly killed. After the coup an Ibo, General Ironsi, emerged as the strongman of the new military government.

The political-tribal balance of power had tilted to the east. The Moslem Hausas were deposed, the Christian Ibos, backed by the army in which fifty percent of the officers were Ibos, were in command. However, the bitter dividing passions remained and a counter coup was inevitable. Ironsi was eventually seized and shot in a new rebellion by northern soldiers, but even before the event anti-Ibo resentment had exploded into bloody riots in the northern city of Kano.

John Okwela hid from the rampaging mobs in the solicitor's office where he was employed. The senior partners were two Indians who barricaded the windows and doors and prayed that they might remain unnoticed. Okwela had also prayed, kneeling with his hands clenched and his eyes tightly closed, pleading with Jesus to protect his wife and children. As soon as the immediate violence had died in the street outside he had persuaded one of the Indians to unbolt the door and let him out. Terrified and desperate he had raced through the darkened mud streets of Kano, back to the *sabon gari*, the stranger's district outside the city walls where the foreigners usually lived.

He was running again in his delirium, his heart was bursting and his lungs were gasping in agony for air. Fear was a red hot barb hooked in his brain and drawing him onward, while black shadows sought to drag him down from recesses and doorways in the blood red walls. Stones and missiles cut and bruised his straining flesh and human animals shrieked and howled at his heels. Again the whole nightmare was painted with the vivid colours of fire and blood.

Somehow he had evaded the hostile crowds and reached the mud-walled house where they had lived. The door was smashed from its hinges and he had stumbled inside to find Victoria dead among the looted ruins of their home. Her clothes were in shreds and one of her breasts had been cut away. The blade of a broken spear had been thrust into her vagina. Of his two sons nothing remained to be found except one severed arm.

The branding iron of memory seared his brain, scarring his heart and blackening his soul. Tears scalded his face and agony and anguish roared through his veins in burning waves. He had drawn the broken spear from his wife's body and screamed again at the vivid rush of blood, in his new vision it rose up and overwhelmed him in a towering wave of gore. In his madness he had charged out into the street to commit more bloody murder, whether he had butchered Hausa, Fulani, Yoruba or Ibo he barely knew. He lived those scenes again in the horrific red world of his fantasies and still he did not know.

He was running again, a hunted fugitive lost in the cruel furnace between sand and sky. The desert roasted him alive, but then he swam rivers of blood and clawed his way out on to banks of flaming bush. Vultures circled on black wings in the crimson sky and he fled shrieking into the fiery forest. Pain and the past were hopelessly twisted into his feverish halucinations and he writhed like a man possessed.

It was later estimated that during the holocaust of northern revenge during October and September of 1966 some thirty thousand Ibo and other easterners were slaughtered. Another million fled the massacres and returned to their tribal homeland in the great forests of the south east.

Eight months later the Ibo governor of the Eastern Region, Lieutenant Colonel Emeka Ojukwu, with a clear mandate from the Ibo consultative assembly, declared the free, sovereign and independent Republic of Biafra.

The newly-emerged head of the Federal Government, Lieutenant Colonel Yakubu Gowon had immediately announced that the rebellion in the east would be swiftly crushed.

John Okwela had not returned to Bumaru. Jesus had not saved his wife and sons and now his own hands were stained with blood. The whole of his past was dead and he was no longer a Christian. The hymn-singing, the Bible reading and the words of the priest were a lie. Jesus did not love him and Jesus had not saved. If there were such things as Gods then the Dark Gods of Africa had proved stronger.

Disillusioned Okwela had joined the army, his university education automatically securing him a commission with the rank of lieutenant. Promotion came fast in times of war and heavy recruiting and within a few months he was made captain.

But the captain had been cut down in his moment of triumph. They had taken Benin and jubilantly swept forward — until the silver demon had shattered his eardrums and the sky rained fire. Ghosts and phantoms ran in howling panic through his tortured dreams. Victoria was dead in the wine-dark lake of her own blood and the tiny arm of his son flew through the air on the blast wings of an explosion. Curtains of flame enveloped his mind as he struggled and screamed against them. Then he was falling, falling, falling into the vast red maw of eternity.

★ ★ ★

Private Awolo heard the captain cry out, and then the thump as the sick man slipped from the back seat to the floor of the jeep. Feeling guilty Awolo glanced back. He had been ordered to drive Okwela to a hospital at Benin or Onitsha, but once clear of the terrifying scene of the ambush he had only one thought in mind. Private Owolo was only a boy and he wanted desperately to get back to his home village and the haven of his mother's mud hut in the heartland of Biafra. Now he had crossed the great bridge over the Niger and was on the road south to Owerri, driving fast on a pitted surface of narrow tarmac through a belt of dense tropical forest. He had almost forgotten the captain and he had no wish to remember.

He wondered if there might be a hospital in Owerri. Perhaps he should stop and look before he drove the last dozen miles to his village. He didn't want to stop but he realized that he must do something about the captain. He twisted in his seat to make a closer inspection of the wounded man huddled on the floor.

Okwela had lost a large amount of blood and the sight of it smeared all over the back seat made Awolo feel ill. Nausea and fear flooded through him again and he pushed his foot even harder against the accelerator.

There was a bend in the road and

Awolo took the corner dead centre and much too fast. He was still looking over his shoulder at Okwela and he crashed the jeep head-on into a short wheel base Land Rover which was approaching from the opposite direction.

* * *

Geoffrey Prescott saw the oncoming jeep with just enough time to stiffen his arms and jerk the Land Rover fiercely to the left. The two vehicles ground together and then tore apart. The Land Rover slid a few yards off the side of the road and then came to a grating stop as Prescott braked with all his strength. The lighter jeep seemed to climb up over the Land Rover's solid offside wing and then tipped on to its side. In a cloud of dust and steam the jeep careered onward, slewing round until it lay broadside across the road. The wheels were still spinning and the engine roared furiously.

Prescott was stunned, but after a

few minutes he was able to get out and walk back. He found Awolo dead with his brains dashed out on the post of the windscreen. Okwela was jammed tightly between the seats, squashed up into the foetal position. Prescott eased him out and found that he was still alive.

3

THE sign read simply: BUMARU MISSION STATION. It pointed down a track which left the main road and continued under a canopy of trees for half a mile before the forest gave way to lush green bush. The sky reappeared blue overhead. Prescott saw the large wooden cross standing high against a froth of white cloud and then the bush parted. The main track circled to the right, behind the mission buildings to where the thatched domed huts of the Ibo village showed like yellow-brown bee hives half-submerged in a sea of banana palms, papayas and cassava.

Prescott stopped the Land Rover on the dusty square before the church, a solid brick building with a thatched roof surmounted by the cross. The wooden doors stood wide open above a flight of concrete steps and in the shadows at the back of the church he could see the image of Christ on a cross behind the white-covered altar. There was no movement inside the church.

On either side there were long brick buildings with thatched roofs and neat wooden verandahs. The building to his right had clinical white curtains at every window, which led him to hope that he had found a small hospital. The building to his left appeared to be divided into more personal rooms. Both buildings and the church were surrounded by flowering gardens, filled with bougainvillaeas, hibiscus and frangipani. Behind the building to his left there was a barrier of eucalyptus trees, giant cottonwoods, and one brilliant flame of the forest. Prescott had more urgent thoughts in mind, but even then he realized that at first sight Bumaru was one of the most beautiful places he had seen in Africa.

Prescott got out of the Land Rover.

A few yards behind him an old Ford truck was parked with the bonnet open. An African youth was tinkering with the engine inside but he pulled his head out to look curiously at Prescott. He wore tattered shorts and an old blue shirt and after a moment he smiled. Prescott started towards him but then there was a movement from the accommodation building as a man moved out on to the verandah. Prescott turned and looked up.

The priest was a surprising figure, a big powerful man with striking blue eyes and a flowing mane of snow-white hair. He appeared to be simply too big for the restraining black robe and the white collar. His movement and the squared-back set of his broad shoulders suggested a strong, forceful personality. Here was no mild-mannered cleric but a thunderer from the Old Testament, a man of God with the purposeful stride of a prophet. He smiled easily to break the imposing spell of his own presence.

"Good day to you, and welcome to Bumaru!" The voice was cheerfully Irish and he rested both hands on the verandah rail in the stance of a ship's captain. "I'm Father O'Keefe. Is there anything I can do to help you?"

"I've got an injured man in the Land Rover," Prescott told him. "He needs help."

The smile faded into a frown and O'Keefe hurried down from the verandah. Prescott opened the back doors of the Land Rover as the priest joined him. The white head leaned forward and the blue eyes stared briefly inside.

"How was he hurt?"

Prescott told him. O'Keefe nodded attentively but turned his head before the Englishman had finished. The African youth who had been working on the truck had moved closer.

"Daniel — " His voice was crisp but not sharp. "Please find Sister Bernadette and Miss Mary. Tell them they are needed here quickly."

The boy nodded and ran off.

O'Keefe turned his attention back to the patient, his big, corded hands feeling gently for broken bones.

"I've already checked him over," Prescott said. "There's no outward injury except the arm."

O'Keefe hesitated, he was not accustomed to having his intentions challenged or restrained. He accepted the calm authority in Prescott's voice but the moment caused him to turn and take stock of his visitor. He saw a tall man wearing denim trousers and a dark green bush shirt that was open at the neck and rolled up at the sleeves. The face was broad with steady grey eyes and creased temples shaded by a battered old bush hat that had seen better days. The face was not handsome but it was strong, not a hard face but definitely not soft. There was no strip of leopard skin around the bush hat, which meant that he did not cater to tourists or his own vanity. O'Keefe sensed suddenly that the character of this man was a threat, some form of subtle danger to himself and the serenity of Bumaru. The thought was a swift, dark and intangible cloud in the back of his mind before he dismissed it as ridiculous.

"I didn't hear your name?" O'Keefe said.

"It's Prescott — Geoffrey Prescott. I'm a historian."

"Studying history, or making it?" O'Keefe asked shrewdly.

Prescott smiled. "I was in the army once, but not any more. And I'm not a mercenary. The civil war is none of my business."

O'Keefe regarded him doubtfully before they were interrupted. The boy Daniel returned at a run with a bustling of nuns and a young blonde girl in a white coat hurrying at his heels. Two of the nuns were young African girls, the third a heavy built white woman in her late fifties with a round dumpling face that had been steamed and yellowed by too many years in an African climate.

When they reached the Land Rover the senior nun and the blonde girl began immediately to examine their patient.

"Mister Prescott assures me there is no sign of injury except the arm," O'Keefe informed them.

The blonde girl straightened up again. She wore her hair drawn back into a short cut pony tail secured with an elastic band. She had a good-shaped face, cheerful and freckled which enabled her to look at her best with the simple hair style, but now she was serious.

"Then we'll take him inside," she decided. "Ruth and Alice, will you make sure the surgery couch is ready, please. And lay out some clean dressings and towels. And boil plenty of hot water."

The two African girls nodded and ran back into the long hospital building.

The white nun emerged from the back of the Land Rover and looked at O'Keefe, her expression one of surprise and deepening concern.

"Liam, it's John Okwela!"

O'Keefe stared at her, and then took a closer look at the grey, pain-ravaged face of the sick man.

"You're right!" His tone echoed her surprise. "In that uniform I didn't recognize him."

"Someone you know?" Prescott asked politely.

"Of course!" The mane of white hair nodded vigorously. "John Okwela was one of our mission boys. He came to us an orphan at two years old. We raised him here at Bumaru." Perplexity deepened the lines on his face. "He was married here. I performed the service in this church. We had letters from him saying that he was practising law in Kano, and his wife had borne him two sons. Now he appears wounded in a military uniform. I do not understand."

"There's a war on." Prescott reminded him in a matter of fact tone. "It changes things for a lot of people."

The priest nodded slowly and his face became unexpectedly bitter.

"We must move him inside," the blonde girl repeated.

Prescott and O'Keefe lifted the unconscious man with ease, Prescott taking the trunk, O'Keefe the head and shoulders. Daniel moved to take the legs once Okwela was clear of the Land Rover and they carried him over to the small hospital. A circle of young African faces had gathered, from toddlers to teenage, but the circle parted quickly to let them through.

Inside the small surgery they laid Okwela carefully on the couch. The nuns and the nurse took over and they backed away. O'Keefe led them back on to the verandah.

"He is in good hands," the priest said. "Sister Bernadette has been with me for ten years. She is a very dear friend, and without her Bumaru would feel a great loss. Miss Mary Kerrigan has been with us for six months, but she too is a very competent young woman. She is a nurse who came to us through the Voluntary Service

Overseas organization."

"How long have you been here?" Prescott asked.

"Twenty years, except for an occasional visit home." O'Keefe smiled. "As a boy I loved Ireland, but I learned to love Africa even more. And I am needed here. God has more work for me in Africa than in Ireland." He paused. "Would you like to see the church and the mission?"

Prescott hesitated. "There's still a job to do. I had to leave the jeep and its driver in the middle of the road."

O'Keefe frowned. "I'll come back with you." He turned to Daniel. "Is the truck ready?"

The boy nodded, he was about sixteen, bright-eyed and eager.

"Yes, Father. I have only to replace the spark plugs."

"Then do it, and call Isaac and Alif. They can help us."

Daniel nodded and trotted down the verandah steps. He went first to the truck where a young African girl of

48

his own age was waiting. The girl wore a bright yellow print dress and stood coquettishly with her hands behind her back. Her hair was a mass of close black curls, similar to the boy's. O'Keefe smiled affectionately towards them.

"That's Rachel, she and Daniel are the oldest of the mission children. Soon it will be time for them to leave us and go out into the world, and we can only pray that we have taught them enough to make them into happy and useful servants to both God and mankind. They are orphans. All the mission children are orphans."

Daniel spoke briefly to the girl and she ran away with the yellow dress swirling brightly around her knees. Light as a butterfly, Prescott thought as he watched her out of sight. Daniel bent his head back inside the engine of the truck and by the time he had finished and lowered the bonnet the girl was back again with two more African youths.

"I think we are ready," O'Keefe said. "If you will lead the way in your Land Rover, I'll follow in the truck with the boys."

★ ★ ★

Mary Kerrigan heard the engines start and watched through the surgery windows as the two vehicles drove away. She wondered briefly where they were going but then turned her attention back to the job in hand. They had fixed up a blood drip to give Okwela an emergency transfusion and then cut away the mess of stained bandages from the injured arm. The wound was long, ragged and deep, a jagged diagonal slash that had opened up the bicep.

"Can we save it?" Mary asked doubtfully.

Sister Bernadette looked up briefly, her eyes calm above her surgical mask. She said quietly,

"We can stop the bleeding and stitch

the wound, and reduce his fever. But only God can save his arm."

She's right, Mary realized. They would do their best but God made the final decisions. She passed Sister Bernadette a swab and took another to wipe the sweat from Okwela's face as the nun began to clean the arm.

My first war wound. The thought flickered through Mary's mind and there was an accompanying shiver in her blood. So far Biafra's civil war had not touched Bumaru, but she knew instinctively that the peace and solitude of the mission could not remain undisturbed. The African soldier on the couch was a bad omen, a pointing finger to a dark future, and suddenly she wished that Prescott had never brought him here. It was an unchristian thought and she was instantly ashamed of it. Mary Kerrigan had been brought up in the Catholic faith, which was her main reason for choosing to work in a Catholic mission, and both as a Catholic and as a nurse her thought was a betrayal.

She had to hold Okwela by the shoulder and elbow as Sister Bernadette closed up the wound and began to sew. If he had been conscious the African would have born the pain with the stoic silence of his race, but unconscious he began to twist and moan, and then to spit curses through his clenched teeth. Ruth Ekwensi and Alice Idoma moved to help restrain him, and the persistent, sinful thought nagged again at Mary's mind.

She knew that dark clouds were gathering over Bumaru.

★ ★ ★

Two hours passed before the Land Rover and the mission truck returned. They had pushed the overturned jeep off the road and recovered the body of Private Awolo. There was no more they could do except telephone the nearest town, which was Owerri, and inform the police and military. By then the harsh red streaks of sunset had daubed the western sky and the evening shadows had lengthened.

"You're welcome to eat with us and stay the night," O'Keefe told Prescott. "I'll get Daniel to show you to our guest bungalow."

Prescott accepted the offer. He had no desire to drive through the night and he was hungry. Daniel led him to a small whitewashed bungalow, one of two neat rows behind the main accommodation building. It was sparsely furnished but spotlessly clean. There was a shower and after Daniel had left Prescott stripped and sluiced away the dust and aches from his body. There was a twinge across his chest as he reached out to turn the shower valve and he remembered the sharper pain when he had started to push the crashed jeep off the road. It was the surprising strength of the priest that had finally moved the vehicle. O'Keefe had the brawn of a blacksmith beneath his black robe, and he had taken command like a general. An extraordinary man, Prescott thought, and mused the words aloud.

He shaved very carefully, and when he had dressed in a clean shirt and slacks there was only the cut on his lip to show any trace of the day's events. He inspected his face in the mirror and was satisfied. There were touches of grey at his temples and a small scar on the lobe of his left ear where a Mau Mau panga had swung perilously close one dark bloody night in the highlands of Kenya, but otherwise he had worn well.

Daniel knocked on the door while he was still brushing his hair and led him back to the main building where dinner was served in the communal dining room.

Prescott found himself seated between Mary Kerrigan and one of the African nuns, Sister Ruth. Father O'Keefe sat at one end of the table and Sister Bernadette at the other. More than a dozen African children, their ages ranging from six to sixteen, made up the company. They had waited for their guest and when Prescott had taken his place O'Keefe turned to one of the older boys.

"Isaac, tonight you can say the prayer."

The whole table bowed their heads. The boy's voice spoke up slowly but clearly:

"Dear Jesus, we thank you for the food on our table. We thank you for our health and our friends. We pray for all your children everywhere. Amen."

"Amen," Prescott said with the chorus. He looked up and saw O'Keefe smiling at him.

"There is no set prayer," the priest said. "We invite the children to take turns in saying their own."

Daniel and Rachel stood up and began to serve the food, a thick savoury stew of meat and vegetables. There were plates of roasted corncobs and cut loaves of bread on the table, together with bowls of mangoes and pitchers of clear water.

"It's not the Ritz," O'Keefe said. "But you won't starve."

"I'm sure I won't." Prescott smiled and turned to the girl beside him. Mary Kerrigan had changed into a simple green dress with a printed pattern of russet ferns. "How is your patient?" Prescott asked.

"He's resting quietly. Sister Alice is watching over him." Mary paused. "We hope that he won't lose his arm."

"We owe you our thanks," Sister Bernadette said sincerely. "I feel sure John must have been trying to return to us." She smiled and her dumpling face took on a cherubic softness.

O'Keefe poured water and broke bread. "You mentioned that you're a historian?" he remarked conversationally.

Prescott nodded. "I served with the Kenya Rifles before independence. Afterwards I stayed on to write a history of East Africa, which proved moderately successful. More recently

56

I've been fascinated by the past civilizations of West Africa, the great empires and kingdoms of Mali, Benin and Kanem-Bornu. I've written a series of articles on each area for the *International Geographic*. Before the war started I was researching a book-length history of Benin."

O'Keefe ate with the steady rhythm of a large, healthy appetite. He stopped and rested his fork.

"I would hesitate to call them civilizations," he objected. "Empires, kingdoms, yes — but they were pagan, barbaric. They were not civilized."

"Yet each society had its own system of government," Prescott answered. "They all passed through cycles of great wealth and power. Kanem-Bornu possessed a huge standing army of negro knights, clothed in chain mail and mounted on horseback."

"But power and riches are not the true essence of civilization."

"Perhaps not," Prescott smiled easily. "But remember that Timbuctoo, as the centre of the Mali empire in the fifteenth century, was famous for its mosques and university. Its merchants made their fortunes carrying books for scholars."

"There is only one important book," O'Keefe said firmly. "And Arab traders carried few Bibles."

"There were other aspects of culture," Prescott insisted. "The Benin sculptors at Ife produced works in bronze which are today regarded as superb examples of African art. While the first Europeans to penetrate Benin were amazed to find a King's Court of galleries and towers which put many of their home towns to shame."

"Armies, books, and primitive face masks in bronze," O'Keefe listed them carelessly. "Put them altogether and still you have no civilization. Benin was a city of blood, built upon human sacrifice and terror. Its Devil's shrines ran red and they built small mountains with the skulls of the victims. Benin was truly a kingdom of darkness."

Prescott shrugged. "Every history has its bloody pages. But Benin only degenerated after the arrival of the white man. The slave trade destroyed Benin, and Europeans were responsible for that. The Oba and his priests only turned to mass slaughter in the last years of despair."

"Medieval Africa was a continent of lost souls." O'Keefe forked a second corncob with an angry thrust and lifted it on to his plate. "The Africans everywhere prayed to fetish spirits," he continued with contempt. "To a tree, a crocodile or a heathen idol. The Ashanti of Ghana worshipped a golden stool."

"Yet every early African society had its own moral order; ceremonies for marriage, to celebrate birth, harvest and the coming of age, and to mourn their dead."

"Pagan ritual," O'Keefe scoffed. "The *Obas* of Benin practised blasphemy and allowed themselves to be worshipped as gods."

"The Pharoahs of Egypt were regarded

as God-Kings," Prescott argued reasonably. "Yet you can hardly deny that they built a mighty civilization."

"How can you compare Benin to Egypt?" Mary Kerrigan risked the question in the hope of diverting them from a quarrel. "The Egyptians built great temples and the pyramids — while I have never heard of Benin!"

"Even so, Benin was a powerful West African nation, capable of raising a hundred thousand warriors to its defence," Prescott informed her. "At its peak it was undoubtedly one of the most important commercial and cultural centres on this part of the globe."

"They were Godless savages," O'Keefe said with increasing impatience.

Prescott smiled, he seemed to be enjoying himself and oblivious to the priest's mood.

"Father, it's a mistake to totally dismiss the early African moral order and their religious beliefs."

"They had no religious beliefs!"

"I must contest that. Most Africans believed in a single God from whom all things flowed. He was the Supreme Being, the Nameless One who was beyond reach."

"The *Oba* sitting on a pile of human skulls!"

"No. On one level the *Oba* was revered as a God-king, but in truth he was the spiritual representative on earth of the Supreme Being. Rather like — " Prescott searched for an illuminating comparison and finished cheerfully: "Rather like the Pope!"

O'Keefe choked over his food.

"The Pope!" Mary Kerrigan repeated in astonishment, she wasn't sure that she had heard correctly.

Prescott nodded. "It's a crude analogy, but it illustrates my meaning. In the same vein the fetish spirits and the spirits of the African ancestors were intermediaries floating half way between this world and the next — like the hierarchy of Catholic saints."

Mary was helplessly silent, while the

African nuns and the listening children looked perplexed.

O'Keefe finished coughing into his napkin and stared at Prescott, a white-maned lion of God who was temporarily uncertain. He simply didn't know whether Prescott was baiting him or not, although the smile was friendly and the man looked serious.

"Your researches must make a fascinating study, Mister Prescott." The calm voice of Sister Bernadette turned the conversation and dissolved the noticeable tension. "Were you working in Lagos?"

"No." Prescott turned his head. "I was staying in Benin City. When the Biafran troops took over it seemed wise to pack my things and get out. I was heading for Port Harcourt and got as far as Owerri when I heard that the Biafrans had moved on and left Benin behind them. I was taking a chance and going back when I hit the jeep."

O'Keefe said doubtfully. "There was a news broadcast on the radio just before we began dinner. The Biafran advance has been stopped and they are falling back upon Benin. It would explain how poor John Okwela became wounded. It may still be unsafe for you to return."

Prescott frowned, this was bad news.

"Do you still have research work to finish?" Sister Bernadette asked him.

"It's not that. The fact-finding is complete and my notes, sketches and so forth are all in the Land Rover. But I was hoping to write the book in Benin, staying on the spot in case any further research did become necessary."

Calmly the nun poured herself a glass of water. "You could stay here," she suggested. "Our guest bungalow is rarely occupied, and you will not find anywhere more peaceful in which to write."

"It's a generous offer," Prescott said. He looked dubiously at the priest.

O'Keefe felt a psychic tremor of warning. Again he sensed that this man was a threat to his peace of mind, but

63

he could not be uncharitable.

"Stay for a few days at least," he said slowly. "Until the war situation becomes more clear."

Prescott thought for a moment, but indecision was not one of his failings. He smiled.

"I accept, and thank you. But you must let me pay for my keep."

"We'll talk about it tomorrow," O'Keefe said.

They resumed their meal but less than a minute passed before Alice Idoma appeared on the verandah. Her black face showed concern inside the white frame of her nun's cowl and she spoke swiftly and urgently to the priest.

"Father, John Okwela is awake."

★ ★ ★

Okwela had emerged from his red dreams into dull pain and dim awareness. He was exhausted, a drained emptiness more vegetable then human. The terrifying images had faded from his mind as though it had been wiped raw to erase even the roots. A shadow leaned over him but was gone before his heart could flutter or his eyes could focus. He realized slowly that he was groaning like a sick animal and clenched his jaws to bring silence.

He opened his eyes and turned his head. He was in darkness but there was a square of paler darkness draped with curtains of black blood. Something nameless choked him and there was panic in his heart. He tried to move but his body had no strength. He was wet with the sweat of fever. There was movement behind him, but turning his head was a slow and painful process and before he could begin a light clicked on. The black blood curtains beyond the window became crimson blossoms of bougainvillaeas. He knew where he was, knowing with a sharp, anguished instinct even before he rolled his head to look at the white-haired priest and the white-cowled nuns.

"It's alright, John." Sister Bernadette rested her hand on his unbandaged arm, her round face smiling serenely down at him. "You're safe with friends. You've returned to Bumaru."

He stared at her. Once the white face had meant love, but now it prompted only hate because she had so cruelly deceived him. The silver crucifix which hung against her breast brought back bitterness and the memory of lies. Jesus did not love! Jesus had not saved! He struggled to withdraw from her loathsome hand.

"No," he croaked. "Not Bumaru. I must leave here. I must go." Panic, fear and desperation surged within him, creating the strength to push up. It was not enough for the big hand of the priest pinned him down like the weight of a mountain.

"You're a sick man," O'Keefe said softly. "You must rest and lie still."

Okwela struggled and screamed. His face contorted as he spat curses and obscenities. Some were in Ibo and some were in English. They pained but did not shock, and when at last he fell back spent the priest and the nun looked at each other with grave faces.

"This hysteria is a bad sign," the nun murmured with foreboding. "His hurt is not confined to his body. He is sick in heart and mind."

"We will pray for him," O'Keefe decided.

The low voices penetrated and Okwela heard. He screamed at them again, his mouth a white-toothed pink wound in the dripping blackness of his face.

"No prayers! Your prayers are curses. I am not a Christian any more. *I do not want you to pray for me!*"

His screams of abuse ebbed into sobs of despair and helpless rage until the last well of his strength was dry. When he became silent he had collapsed back into unconsciousness.

4

AS Brad Tucker had so casually observed, the air war was hotting up. By the end of August Federal Nigeria had thirteen jet combat aircraft operational and the mercenary pilots were flying from dawn to dusk. Their targets were army camps, troop convoys, radio masts and power stations, although the South Africans were not above dropping any spare bombs on to any bunch of 'bloody kaffirs' who strayed into their sights. The Biafrans themselves had blown up the great bridge at Onitsha to cover their retreat back across the Niger, but many others were destroyed from the air.

The pilots flew by day and drank by night, in the hotel bars of Lagos, Kano or Kaduna, or wherever they happened to be. Maxwell and Tucker followed the general pattern, despite the crystallizing doubts in Maxwell's mind. They needed beer to replace the day's lost sweat and slake the internal dust, and bourbon to dull the nagging voice of conscience.

"It's not my kind of war, Brad," Maxwell confessed gloomily.

They were sitting in their regular hotel bar in Kano, close to the open window. Outside the night air was hot and windless, filled with the musky smell of Africa, a blend of dust, the odour of goats and the fragrance of frangipani. The hotel beer garden beyond the window was surrounded by a crenellated mud wall and shaded by a single tall jacaranda. A blue-grey ghecko some eight inches long with a bright orange head was frozen as though crucified to the trunk of the tree and Maxwell was staring into its bright black eyes.

"I figured," Tucker said. "You haven't been the same old Smiling Hank just lately. Seems like you found

the old smile and then lost it again."
He took a long pull at his beer and
then glanced at the occupied table on
the far side of the room. "Those guys
bug you?"

Maxwell nodded slowly, without
disengaging from his staring match
with the lizard. He had watched the
rival party enter: Culik and Assab,
with two more Czechs and another
Egyptian who were nameless. They
had never been introduced. Escorting
the party was the ostentatious Colonel
Black, whose role now appeared to be
that of general watchdog. The Czech
and Egyptian pilots made only rare
public appearances, but when they did
the African in the maroon suit was
always there.

"Not only them," Maxwell said. "It's
the whole set-up. In Korea every other
flight ended in a dog-fight. We knew
what we were fighting, and we were
hitting an enemy who could hit back.
Here we're just hammering a bunch of
ignorant blacks on the ground."

"Biafra's getting more and more artillery," Tucker cautioned. "Ojukwu's spending money on arms as fast as he can grab up the cash. He knows it's only a matter of time before Gowon gets smart and makes the old Nigerian pound worthless by issuing new currency. And the rumours are that he's getting a dozen aircraft from the French. You could see a few dog-fights yet!"

"No chance." Maxwell said cynically. "If Biafra gets those French planes they'll have to hire pilots to fly them. They'll be white mercenaries, just the same as us. They'll be flying for hard cash, not to risk their lives, so they'll avoid any risk of a dog-fight. We'll all play it nice and safe and stick to dropping bombs on the black buggers in the bush."

"Is that so bad? We didn't come out here to get killed."

"No." Maxwell scowled at the lizard and abruptly its unblinking gaze snapped away. The reptile scuttled round the curve of the tree trunk and was hidden from sight. Maxwell turned his attention to Tucker.

"Things have changed, Brad. This is a different kind of war, or maybe I'm a different kind of man. Korea was simple. Communism was taking over by force and we were there to stop them. We were fighting to give the people out there a chance to live a decent, American kind of life. I guess for most Americans that brand of simplicity got shot to pieces in Vietnam, although I didn't think about it much at the time. Now I am thinking, but I'm not sure of what we're doing. We're flying on the same side as Mig 17s, and the ground forces we're protecting are equipped with Russian arms."

"You have to forget that. In this war just about every arms dealer on both sides of the iron curtain is making as many sales as he can, and none of them give a damn whether they sell to the Federals or Biafra or both."

"Sure, it's a scramble to get rich.

That's why I don't feel we're stopping anything bad out here, or preserving anything necessarily good. Maybe the Biafrans have a right to secede, and we're just making a tribal battle bloodier."

"Forget it," Tucker insisted again. "If we quit tomorrow, Colonel Black will hire two more pilots and nothing will have changed. Just remember that if this war lasts for a few more months we'll be able to buy back one of the Dakotas. Maybe we can go back to Kansas and start Max-Air all over again."

"No deal. No more Max-Air and no more Kansas." Maxwell was positive but then he relaxed and grinned. "This time we'll call it Tucker Airlines and start up in Tennessee."

"I'll drink to that."

Tucker emptied his glass. Maxwell crooked a finger to signal a waiter and ordered two more. Voices sounded outside and Lou Hendrix strolled in with two more South Africans.

"Make it five," Maxwell told the waiter. "Five beers, and five slugs of whisky."

"Yes, sir. Right away, sir." The African youth glanced left and right and then hurried back to the bar. He was suddenly nervous and Maxwell knew why.

Hendrix slumped down, his heavy bulk overflowing the cane chair. He tugged off another button from his shirtfront to reveal more of a grey-haired chest and his brick-red face relaxed in a lazy grin.

"Beer and whisky, sounds good, man. Maybe I'll try that mixture."

The others laughed, their diet never changed. They drank the same and talked the same regardless of their surroundings. Jan Hollard and his friend Van der Walt piloted two more of the Delfin L 29s as a team and went unprompted into an account of their day's work.

"We hit this army camp near Enugu," Hollard said cheerfully. "There must have been a full division going through some training tactics. They had a bunch of white officers — "

"Frenchmen," Hendrix said. "I heard Ojukwu's hired a couple of hundred French mercenaries to train his troops. Most of them old Congo hands."

"Maybe. Anyway, we caught them right in the open. You should have seen those kaffirs run, man, like a herd of bloody bushbuck when a lion rips out a jugular. They ran in all directions. We must have killed a hundred."

"We took out a power station," Hendrix said. "They had some artillery but Hank goes through it like they're chucking up confetti as a welcome."

"No point in hanging around," Maxwell shrugged. "I like to get through that stuff as fast as possible." He could have told them what it had been like in Korea, where the stuff came up in a solid wall instead of isolated squirts, but he didn't. The war talk bored him, and he was beginning to realize that Hendrix was the only one of the South African pilots he didn't actively dislike. They drank together because they were thrown together by profession and circumstance, but that was all. The drinks came and he lifted the glasses off the tray and pushed them across the table.

"Cheers, man." Hendrix poured a long swallow down his throat.

Hollard did the same. "Here's to more dead kaffirs."

Maxwell signed a chit for the waiter. The act that he didn't share the toast went unnoticed. Van der Walt put down his glass and took up the original story.

"We took a few bullet holes as we dived. Somebody down there had a bofors gun and kept his nerve. One of the Frenchies, I guess. A black would have run. Anyway it was — "

He paused. Hollard was looking over his shoulder and Hollard was smiling. Releasing his glass Hollard began to tap out a gentle rhythm on the table top. He used one fingernail but it was suddenly loud in the silence. Hendrix and van der Walt turned their heads to follow the line of Hollard's gaze, and they too began to grin.

Here it comes, Maxwell thought wearily. The cold war, round what? He had forgotten. The tapping was taken up by the other two South Africans. The beat quickened and became lively. On the far side of the room the hawk-nosed Major Assab and his Arab companion sat stiff and rigid. The Czechs looked angry and the negro face of Colonel Black was turning purple with barely restrained fury.

The tune was a calculated insult to the Egyptians and a cruel embarrassment to their allies. The South Africans began to sing, or more accurately to bawl out the words in chorus. The song was the Jewish national anthem.

A glass and a chair crashed over as Assab pushed himself violently to his feet. He started to turn but then Vlado Culik grasped his wrist and jerked him back. The second Arab had jumped up but less certainly. Assab glared down and the young Czech shook his blonde head in warning.

The singing stopped. Van der Walt shifted his chair. The three South Africans were ready, grinning and waiting. Assab was trembling.

"Major, please." Colonel Black had swallowed his rage and pride, even though the effort had almost choked him, and he struggled to bring the situation under control. He had his values as a diplomat for he continued his plea for restraint in Arabic.

The two Egyptians refused to sit down and Assab remained hostile. Chairs scraped as the rest of the group stood up and Culik and the two Czechs moved to form a tactful barrier between the Arabs and the table where the South Africans and the two Americans were still seated. Their African host now gripped an Egyptian arm in each hand and with difficulty steered his charges to the door. The Czechs followed without looking back.

The song began again, a triumphant shout. Assab twisted to look over his shoulder but then he was hustled out. His dark face was apoplectic and there was murder in his eyes.

"It never fails," Hollard laughed. "Man, it never fails!"

Hendrix grinned and beckoned to the waiter. "Five more beers and five more whiskies. We're celebrating. It's my dog's birthday!"

★ ★ ★

The following morning they were airborne at dawn, flying south to Biafra with the horizon red as blood below the port wingtip. The new day, like the newly emerging Africa, was beginning with a baptism of fire. In less than an hour they crossed the Benue River at thirty-five thousand feet, one hundred miles east of its junction with the Niger. South of the Benue the rain forest began, the bush becoming more lush, vast lakes of green merging into

79

a green sea of foliage waves.

They were four Delfin L 29s. The Mig 17s would take off later keeping their own company. Even in the air there was careful segregation. Perhaps that was just as well, Maxwell thought grimly. In the heat of battle it was just possible he would turn on a Mig like a snapping dog in a mongrel pack. He felt no deep hostility for the Czech and Egyptian pilots, it was the Migs which stuck in his gullet and brought the sour taste to his mouth.

The battle lines were marked by puff balls of black smoke and, as they dropped height, by the crump of explosions. The Federal advance on the Biafran capital of Enugu was being held back by stubborn resistance and several troop divisions were tangled in fierce fighting. The bloodshed was discreetly shielded by the thick canopy of forest and only the smoke stains, the occasional blazing vehicle along the only road, and the excited babble from the radio gave evidence to its ferocity.

It took a few minutes to sort out the garble of directions and co-ordinates from below, then Maxwell pressed his speech button.

"Delfin Leader to Delfin Wing. It sounds as though the Federals are mainly on the west side of the road, the Biafrans on the east. There's one Biafran defensive position about a mile south on the Federal side with a battery of field guns. I'll take that one. The rest of you strafe the east side."

He heard their acknowledgement and then tilted the nose down in a long dive. He flew a parallel course on the west side of the road, searching ahead and to his right. Tucker would search left, it was their routine procedure. The jungle rushed up to meet them, broken by clearings, some marked by fire and others filled with scattering men as the jet howled over their heads. A few of the braver souls stood up and waved, confident that air power was on their side. Within seconds they were over the friendly lines.

"Ahead left!" Tucker said sharply.

Maxwell twisted his head and saw the muzzle flashes and smoke puffs coming from the next clearing. The enemy field guns were screened with vegetation and netting on the edge of the forest but they had betrayed themselves. He didn't hear the shells explode as he banked the jet to port in a steeply descending attack. He was conscious of a machine gun blazing into his sights as he fired both wing batches of rockets. He dropped his bomb load and pulled the jet into a climb. When he looked down over his shoulder the bombs were exploding smack on target. It was all too easy.

He looked east of the road and saw the remaining three Delfins finishing off their attack. They were mopping up with cannon fire. He used the radio again.

"Delfin Leader to Delfin Wing. Let's go home. We'll be late for breakfast."

★ ★ ★

They returned to find that Kano airport was once more an ant's nest of feverish activity, although this time it came as no surprise. A whole fleet of at least fifteen of the giant Russian Ilyushins had landed and were busily unloading arms, ammunition and more Mig jets. The four Delfins landed close by and taxied to a stop. Maxwell was the last to land and when he and Tucker climbed down on to the runway only Hendrix was waiting for them.

"The boys figured the Russians might drink all the coffee," Hendrix said.

Maxwell grinned. "If they swallow as much vodka as you drink whisky, they probably need it."

Hendrix laughed, he had a simple sense of humour that was easily touched off. They fell into step and walked towards the main block of buildings. Tucker unwrapped a caramel and flipped it into his mouth. A fuel truck hurried past to top up their aircraft for the next flight, which would be immediately after they had eaten. It swirled up a cloud of dust.

"It looks like we're getting too much help." Hendrix jerked his thumb towards the unloading operation. "If they fly in any more jets we'll finish this war much too soon. I need at least another six months before I can buy my farm."

"You got somewhere in mind?" Maxwell asked.

"Sure, man. In the Transvaal, up on the northern veld. On the high ground its good cattle grazing. I know a place coming up for sale within a year and I've got first option if I can raise the rand."

"I didn't know you were a farmer," Tucker said.

"I'm not, but when this is over I intend to make a start. I'm not an air ace any more. This job is a soft touch but I'm still getting too many grey hairs. I got myself married six months ago, left my wife in Pretoria, she wants — "

Hendrix broke off and never finished.

They all heard the sound of approaching aircraft and turned their heads to the south. They were expecting nothing more sinister than the daily Nigerian Airways flight from Lagos, but almost immediately they realized that there were two planes, both streaking up fast from below the southern horizon. Maxwell stared and then recognition dawned and complacency vanished. The planes were Biafra's two ancient B 26 bombers.

"Goddamn! It's a raid!" Maxwell roared the warning and turned to run. Instinct told him to get far away from the unloading area where the Russian Ilyushins sat helpless like great, fat sitting ducks. As a target they were better than a magnet.

Tucker sprinted at Maxwell's heels, pausing only to spit out his half chewed toffee. As he did so he saw that Hendrix was heading the wrong way.

"Lou!" Tucker yelled.

Maxwell skidded to a stop and looked back. Hendrix was racing for his Delfin and it was obvious what he had in mind. The South African was reacting with the instinct of a veteran of World War Two, aiming to get his ship airborne and give battle to the enemy. Except that this wasn't the Battle For Britain, Maxwell thought with frustration. A penny-ante punch-up in Africa wasn't worth getting killed over.

"Lou, come back you damned fool!"

Maxwell added his voice to Tucker's but both were lost in the deafening thunder as the bombers swept overhead. Maxwell hauled on his helmet as he threw himself forward and hit the deck. Dust clouded into his mouth and nose and the earth shook as the bombs came down. The crack of the explosions tore at his eardrums and his heart pounded as he cowered to the dirt. He had forgotten just how bad it was to be this close. Tucker sprawled beside him but his eyes were fixed on Hendrix. One second the South African had been still running and the next he was driven sideways as though he had taken a mighty swipe across the middle with an iron baseball bat.

Maxwell scrambled up with Tucker beside him. Flames crackled and men were shouting and screaming from the centre of the unloading area where a pall of black smoke was already blanketing the scene. The two Americans ignored it and reached Hendrix.

The South African had rolled into a bloody heap with both hands clutching his belly. One look was enough to tell Maxwell that he had stopped a large chunk of flying shrapnel.

"Let's get him under cover," Tucker said hoarsely.

Maxwell nodded and lifted Hendrix by the shoulders. Tucker took his feet and they made a staggering run towards the nearest building. Half way there they realized that the bombers had departed and were not intending to return. They stopped and lowered Hendrix gently to the earth.

By then Hendrix was dead.

There was sweat, dust and shock on Tucker's face. Suddenly he was just a bald old man with shaking fat. Maxwell wondered whether he looked as bad. He certainly didn't feel any too good. Neither of them had anything to say.

5

THE war had still not reached Bumaru. Life at the mission went on much as before except for the sound of Prescott's typewriter tapping briskly from the verandah of the guest bungalow. Mary Kerrigan and Sister Bernadette tended the sick, treating those who trekked in daily from the surrounding bush in the small surgery, delivering babies and nursing the bad cases in the hospital beds. Sister Alice and Sister Ruth taught simple lessons in the long, open-sided schoolroom behind the church, the seriousness of the classroom frequently punctuated by laughter and singing. O'Keefe preached and led holy services, helped out wherever he was needed and generally orchestrated the happy whole. He wielded hammer, spanner or spade all with the same dynamic energy. He had built Bumaru with only African help. His big hands had sawn every timber and laid every brick. He had planned the flower and vegetable gardens which the older mission boys now planted and hoed and he was pleased with his work. He hoped, humbly, that God would continue to smile upon Bumaru.

Okwela was growing stronger, a surly and uncommunicative patient but his arm was healing. The arm would never be the same again, it was a permanent weakness he would have to bear like a withered badge, but his body strength was returning. He had decided bitterly that his left arm was another debt to be added to Victoria and his two sons. Soon he would collect payment, in Yoruba, Hausa and Fulani blood.

He had refused to talk to the priest and the nuns, knowing his rejection caused them pain. He didn't care. He had grown up. He was not a stupid mission boy any more. He was embarrassed because he owed them another debt, but then he told himself that he had never asked for anything. They had always given because they wanted his soul for Jesus. He owed them nothing.

As soon as he was able he spent most of his time on the hospital verandah. He couldn't stand the atmosphere of antiseptic and sickness inside the building and he hated the close proximity of his fellow patients. The old man with his lungs riddled with tuberculosis who coughed incessantly and hawked blood revolted him, and he was frankly terrified of the ulcerated *thing* in the end bed. He knew the disease was yaws, but whether the victim was male or female he had never dared to find out.

Mary Kerrigan had set out a cane chair for him, in the shade facing the church, but Okwela had moved it round to the end of the building where he could look away from the shadow of the cross. He preferred to roast in the full heat of the sun. He

91

had refused to be taken inside the church and when he heard the sound of voices raised in worship he gritted his teeth with anger and strove to close his ears. Every hymn was a monstrous mockery, and he knew they persisted in praying for him despite his constant denial of their futile faith.

He sat one morning with a book lying unopened at his feet. Alice Idoma had left the book but Okwela wanted nothing from the nuns and would not read it. Instead he watched Daniel at work on a flower bed a few yards away. The boy wore only shorts and plimsoles and had his back bent to the job as he raked carefully between the blooms. On a sudden impulse Okwela stood up and approached him.

Daniel sensed his presence, straightened up and turned. He smiled uncertainly into Okwela's glowering eyes.

"How old are you?" Okwela demanded. He was not prepared to waste time on greetings and preliminaries. "Sixteen," Daniel answered.

"Old enough to fight," Okwela said contemptuously. "Yet Biafra is at war and needs soldiers — while you weed flowers at a white man's mission. What are you? Woman or child?"

Daniel's jaw dropped. His heart suddenly hammered and the hot blood of embarrassment rushed to his face. The attack had caught him off guard and the intensity of Okwela's eyes made him squirm.

"I am not a soldier," he stammered, and the words sounded stupid even to his own ears. "I do not know how to fight."

"Then you should learn!" Okwela whipped him with words. "Learn before the Hausas come to cut off your testicles! Learn before the Fulani come to rape your pretty girl friend in the yellow dress, before they slice off her breasts and slit open her belly! Learn before the Yoruba come to slaughter the Ibo children! All this will happen because I have seen it happen in other places. Biafra must win this war, and

93

you should join the army and fight! You and any other boys who are old enough to carry a rifle. The prayers of the priest are not enough to save you."

"How can I leave?" the boy protested. "This is my home."

"You will have no home when the enemies of Biafra burn these buildings to the ground. Go to Enugu and join the army before it is too late."

Daniel gripped the handle of his rake until his black knuckles showed white. He did not know what to say. He was ashamed, whether it was because he did not want to fight or because he did not know how to answer he did not know. Okwela saw his shame and was enraged.

"Do you think that I do not want to fight?" Okwela screeched. "It is only my arm which keeps me here. As soon as I am fit I shall return to the war. I am a Captain, my place is with my soldiers."

The fist of his right hand was clenched and for a moment he wanted to strike out and hit this pathetic, hymn-fed imitation African. He took a faltering step forward and felt weak at the knees. He was suddenly dizzy and knew that even though the fever had retreated it had left a hollow man in its wake. He wanted to sob with frustration and struggled to hold back the tears.

"Come back to the verandah," Mary Kerrigan said from behind him. "Come back before you fall down."

He turned and saw her through a mist. The Irish nurse was the only member of the mission staff with whom he had talked, because she was not a nun, and she knew nothing of his childhood at Bumaru. But he had only asked her for reports on the war, nothing else. Now she took his arm as though that gave her some prior claim and pulled him away. Her grip was strong, emphasizing his weakness, and he could not resist.

"Stay there," Mary said as she returned him to his chair. "And if you can't be grateful for what we're doing for you, at least be silent."

There was anger in her tone, a hint of Irish temper, and suddenly Okwela hated her as much as the others. His eyes blazed and he was sweating. This white bitch in the white coat had humiliated him in front of the boy. One day it would be his turn to hurt her, but not today.

"I don't understand you," Mary continued in exasperation. "After all we've done for you you're still sullen and resentful."

"Your people have never understood mine," Okwela accused hoarsely. "You come to Africa to teach us, to change us, but not to understand. You care nothing for what we are — only for what you want us to be."

Mary stared down at him. For a moment she was hesitant, almost afraid, and then her training took over. "That's pure nonsense," she told him briskly. She picked up the book he had ignored and slapped it down on his knee. "Just get on with your reading and behave yourself."

She walked away and left him seething.

★ ★ ★

"Olduvai — " O'Keefe said with distaste a week later. His tone was wary because his after-dinner conversations with Prescott had formed a disconcerting habit of following uncomfortable tracks. He could not reconcile with many of Prescott's views, even though the man was undoubtedly knowledgeable about physical Africa. "Have you been there?"

Prescott nodded and leaned back with his coffee. This was the time of evening when he liked to talk.

"During my time in Kenya." He stirred his cup lazily. "They gave us some leave from chasing Mau Mau, and most of them I spent the way soldiers usually spend their free time. But twice I made visits to the gorge.

97

It was there I first became interested in the early history of Africa."

"Olduvai Gorge," Mary Kerrigan repeated in an effort to remember. "Isn't that an archaeological site in Tanzania?"

"It's where Leakey discovered the skull of an apeman who walked upright two million years ago," Prescott told her. "He had a large brain case and used pebble chopping tools, and he's a strong contender for the missing link between our own stone-age ancestors and gorillas in the jungle. His bones and the tools he used were preserved in layers of river sediment and volcanic ash."

"Surely you don't believe in the false doctrines of evolution?"

Prescott turned his head to look at O'Keefe.

"I believe in logic and the weight of scientific evidence." He smiled. "It may be difficult to accept that out distant grandfathers sprang from the loins of an African ape, but since Darwin there's been no credible alternative."

"God created Adam in the Garden of Eden," O'Keefe spoke in the voice of the pulpit. *"He formed man of the dust of the ground, and breathed into his nostrils the breath of life; and man became a living soul.* There is your alternative. You should read Genesis!"

"I have read the Bible, and the Koran, the Upanishads and a few others. They all carry a certain amount of dead weight; mythology to fill in the unknown, and parables useful to illlustrate a point but never intended as a factual account. Surely nobody takes the Garden of Eden literally any more?"

"The Bible is the Word of God," O'Keefe said forcefully. "It carries no dead weight. It has brought, and still brings, peace and comfort to uncounted multitudes of human beings."

"The Bible is a very valuable book," Prescott agreed. "But basically it is still the mythology and history of the Jews, the biographies of a collection of prophets, and of one very holy man who was the Son of God inasmuch as we are all the sons of God."

O'Keefe stared at him. He was tempted to launch into a sermon but he knew it would have no effect. Sometimes he wondered whether Prescott deliberately sought to offend him, or whether the man simply did not realize that most of his opinions were anathema. During the few short weeks that Prescott had been resident at the mission his presence and influence had been almost as disturbing as that of John Okwela. O'Keefe was convinced that something terrible had happened to Okwela to destroy his faith and he was deeply concerned. With Prescott he wondered whether the man had ever possessed any faith of any kind. Prescott talked like a man who had read widely for knowledge, as though learning was more important than faith.

"Jesus Christ is the only Son of God." O'Keefe stated his own faith bluntly. "I have always believed in the Bible and lived by its laws. My life has been happy, and I hope a useful one."

"I'm sure it has, Father. And I won't deny the ten commandments as positive guidelines for everyone. But the Bible can be taken too literally, to sanction evil. The horrors of the Spanish inquisition, the wars of the crusades, the mass slaughter of the Aztec, Inca and Toltec peoples in South America, were all blessed by priests in the name of God."

"A priest is only a man. And like all men we have fallen from grace through original sin. Perhaps it is inevitable that we shall make some mistakes as we seek to return."

"So we're back to Eden and the original sin." Prescott smiled. "I very much suspect that Eden was somewhere like the Olduvai Gorge, and the original sin was not an apple eaten by Adam, but the rock which he first picked up to dash out his neighbour's brains. It was the discovery of the weapon which set man above the other animals, ensured his evolution, and doomed him to an eternity of wars and strife."

"Was it bad in Kenya?" Mary changed the subject quickly. She could see an argument brewing and although they had always kept their differences civil she feared the priest would eventually explode. Prescott was a stiff-necked boor throwing out a blind challenge with every other word.

"Bad enough." Prescott switched the flow of his thoughts with practised ease. "Eight years of terror, settlers murdered, farms burned, livestock butchered, and thousands of Africans put to death. For me it meant months on end in the Aberdares, hunting men and being hunted. There were experiences I don't want to repeat."

"A sad and horrible story," Sister Bernadette remarked quietly. "It's difficult to believe that Kenya was the most advanced area of Africa, where the Christian missions had performed some of their greatest work."

"The Kikuyu lost sight of God," O'Keefe said. "They reverted to darkness and pagan ceremonies."

"They fought in the only way possible to throw out an alien white society which had occupied their lands and treated them with contempt." Prescott contradicted with his usual relaxed obstinacy. "After two world wars had shown them that the European was not a superior moral being with an all-powerful God, their revolt was a natural process of history. Colonialism had to end. Independence had to come."

Prescott drank the last of his coffee, then concluded. "It was precisely because the Kikuyu were among the best educated of the African tribes that they were the first to rebel. They had the longest exposure to the contradictions of European values. They were the first to become aware that their white masters were just another human race with all the usual divisions and weaknesses."

"But why did they reject God?"

"Because they realized that what was preached in the missions was not practised by every white man they met."

"But the filth of Mau Mau was not necessary."

Prescott shrugged. "Mau Mau was bloody but it was not all mindless savagery. It had its positive aims."

"It was an abomination against God. They turned to blood sacrifice, oath-taking and the most revolting practices the mind can imagine. Their secret rites were an orgy of evil."

"All means to an end. The white man took away the black man's identity, both political and spiritual. We tried to erase his culture and even his racial memory, but it was something that couldn't happen. Eventually the African had to re-assert himself. Kenya was the beginning, then Tanzania, Congo — "

"And now Nigeria." O'Keefe saw the trend of his thought.

Prescott smiled and nodded. "Here the British left behind a political monolith

104

they shaped to suit themselves, but the ethnic groups of Africa will forge their own destiny, as Biafra is attempting now."

"Do you support the new republic?" O'Keefe asked.

"My support is irrelevant," Prescott said wryly. "The future of Africa can only be decided by the Africans."

O'Keefe nodded agreement, for politics was less volatile than religion. "You are right, of course, but it is a tragedy that nothing can be decided without bloodshed."

"Nothing ever has." Prescott shrugged. "Perhaps nothing ever will. Deep down man's instincts have not changed for two million years. He's more sophisticated, more knowledgeable, and he's made great technological achievements, but basically he's still a predator, jealous of his own territory and determined to dominate his neighbours."

"Two thousand years ago man was given a wonderful new opportunity; Perhaps even now its not too late to hope that eventually — "

O'Keefe stopped and raised his head. Mary Kerrigan had been listening for the last minute, first to the excited barking of a dog in the village, and then to the distant chatter of voices which had now added to the general discord.

"Something's happening." Prescott said.

O'Keefe stood up and walked on to the verandah. Mary and Sister Bernadette followed. Prescott remained alone at the table, the dishes had been cleared and their African companions had dispersed before the conversation began. There was fear mixed like dark smoke in the wind of the distant voices, and slowly Prescott stood up and moved to join the others.

O'Keefe was staring past the black silhouette of the church, trying to penetrate the darkness that shrouded the village beyond. It was a moonless night with no stars, filled with the insect symphony played by invisible wings. The hot air was still and yet it droned with hidden vibrations, leaves rustled, and a lizard scuttled in the dry thatch overhead. Mary jumped, as though it might have been a snake, and unconsciously Prescott rested a reassuring hand on her arm.

Bare feet pounded on the hard-baked earth. Someone was running and breathing fast. Daniel appeared and stopped, the whites of his eyes rolling upward in his black face.

"Father," he gasped. "Many people have come to the village. They have walked from Enugu. They say Enugu has been captured by the Federal soldiers and there has been much killing. They had to flee for their lives. Some of them are hurt."

★ ★ ★

They met the first trickle of refugees coming up through the huts from the village, a dozen Africans, tired and footsore with shocked, scared faces.

The men carried baskets and hastily gathered bundles of possessions in their arms, while the women balanced larger bundles on their heads. Their children stumbled miserably beside them and one woman carried a baby on her back. The men talked all at once and one of them gestured repeatedly to the blood-stained bandage around his head. Mary Kerrigan moved to examine him but then Prescott pulled her back.

"He can wait, he'll live," Prescott said. And then before her temper could rise and she could argue, "Here's your first patient."

Mary stared at the young Ibo woman Prescott had pulled forward. The girl looked unharmed except for the expression of dull anguish engraved deep on her face. Then Mary looked more closely at the bundle in the girl's arms. It was not just another bundle of household items. It was a child wrapped in a grey blanket. She moved the blanket and saw that one small leg ended in a knot of bloody bandages just below the knee.

Mary felt sick. Tropical disease, swollen bellies, gangrene and all the horrors induced by the climate she could bear, but the child's foot had been blown off by a shell, made in a factory, sold for hard cash and fired in cold blood. That was sickening. It made men more repellent than the crawling worms, parasites and microbes that were the front line enemy of her profession.

"Get the surgery ready. I'll bring the child."

Prescott was cool and efficient as he took the child from its mother, and suddenly Mary was angry with him too. Then she realized that O'Keefe and the nuns were equally calm, although she could read the pain in their eyes. O'Keefe quickly restored order and she hurried ahead to the hospital. Prescott followed with Sister Bernadette and the young Ibo woman who refused to be left behind.

Prescott laid the child on the operating table and peeled back the stained blanket. The child was female, perhaps four or five years old, unconscious and near to death. Her pulse was difficult to find. Her face was grey and wasted. Mary pulled on a face mask and rubber gloves and pushed Prescott aside. Sister Bernadette joined her and they worked swiftly to connect up plasma and saline flasks with rubber tubes and needles to the thin arms.

Prescott stepped back. He was in the way now and turned to leave the surgery. He bumped into the young Ibo woman who was staring dumbly at the surgery table. Gently he moved her back to the door but she would go no further. She looked into his eyes for a moment and then squatted defiantly in the doorway.

"Let her stay," Sister Bernadette had glanced over her shoulder. "She won't interfere."

Prescott nodded and went out.

Okwela heard the disturbance and raised himself upon his right elbow. He listened hard, recognizing the English voice of the priest as O'Keefe organized food and shelter, and then the fragments of broken news carried on Ibo tongues. The words formed meaning, injecting him with fear and anguish. The enormity of disaster washed over him in a giant wave and without any conscious decision he struggled out of his bed.

He heard the nurse and the nuns bring a patient into the surgery at the end of the ward. He was still for a moment and when he moved again it was with stealth and silence. He found his clothes in the locker beside his bed and began to dress, fumbling with trousers and boots, and his army shirt and tunic which had been removed by the nuns and then returned cleaned with the left sleeves cut neatly away. The old man with tuberculosis coughed noisily in the next bed. Okwela cursed him and glanced fretfully to the surgery door where bars of light now showed at top and bottom. His enemies were busy in there, and he hoped they were too busy to take notice of an old man's cough.

He walked slowly down the ward, conscious of dark, pain-filled eyes fixed on his passing figure. Most of the patients were awake, but none betrayed him. He went through the far door and out on to the verandah. Two minutes later he was on the jungle track which led back to the main road. He hurried with the wrist of his left hand tucked inside his open tunic for support.

He was needed at the battlefront. It was time to find his unit.

* * *

For forty minutes the small life fluttered like a candle flame on the edge of extinction. The tiny lips turned blue, regained colour and turned blue again. The faint pulse faded and twice Mary believed that it had gone forever. Twice it came back, feeble and intermittent against her fingertip. Mary could feel the sweat trickle down her temples and soak into her mask. She saw the same gleams of perspiration above the worn grey eyes of Sister Bernadette as the nun prepared and administered an injection. The pulse beat strengthened. Mary tried to smile with her eyes. Her throat was too dry to speak. She wanted to swab the moisture from both their faces but the blood flask was empty and needed changing. The African nuns who normally helped were busy treating lesser injuries on the verandah.

They cut away the soiled tourniquet from the purple swollen stump, exposing a mess of blood, pus, dirt and splintered bone. Mary bit her lip beneath her mask. She was a nursing sister, not a surgeon, but the nearest surgeon was probably in Lagos. They had to do what they were able. The nun led the way, injecting an anaesthetic, cleaning out the dirt and splinters, draining the pus and sawing off the jagged edges of bone. Finally the loose folds of flesh were sewn together, the stump was bandaged and injected with penicillin against infection. When it was over Mary's hands began to shake. The nun smiled. The second bottle of blood plasma was almost empty and the child was alive.

They stripped off their gloves and masks. Sister Bernadette looked old and tired. Mary turned to see whether Alice or Ruth were available to put the patient to bed and saw that the child's mother was still squatting in the doorway. They had forgotten the young Ibo woman who had waited so patiently, and now it appeared that she had fallen asleep. Her curly black head had tilted sideways against the doorpost.

Mary smiled and went to her.

"It's alright. You can wake up now. Your little girl is going to live."

She touched the Ibo woman's shoulder and her smile froze. The mother had simply rolled sideways and lay still. Where she had been squatting the floorboards were wet with a large red pool of blood.

Sister Bernadette knelt beside her and pushed back the dead woman's dress. There were livid bruise marks on her stomach but no wound.

"Internal haemorrhage," the nun said quietly. "God rest her soul."

"Why didn't she tell us?" Mary demanded. She felt guilty, almost angry, because they had not realized that the woman was bleeding. "We might have saved her."

"Her child was more important, so she waited." Sister Bernadette understood and her voice was infinitely sad. She was accustomed to the uncomplaining patience of African mothers. She stood up and turned to Mary. Compassion served only the living and she could see strain and disillusion in the younger girl's eyes.

"You should rest," she said gently. "Try not to think about it. I fear this is only the beginning."

6

THE war dragged on; through the rainy season when the skies opened up with torrential sheets of crashing water, when the jungle steamed and the roads became rivers of red mud; through the dry season when the sun baked the earth and the bush and the forest; and on to the beginning of the next rains. Biafra shrank to half its size as the Federal forces savaged the infant republic with their sheer weight of numbers and the brand new weapons and armoured cars poured in belatedly by the British to counter the growing influence of the Russians with their massive shipments of bombers and bombs. The civil war was the first ever to be fought between Africans with modern weapons, and it was an elusive, shifting, savage and bloody affair. Inexorably Biafra lost ground, and the conquered areas were marked by the black wings of circling vultures, the stink of rotting and roasting corpses, and the smoke and flames of the burning villages. Despite all the fine platitudes voiced in Lagos the terrible tribal hatreds left no room for compassion and rehabilitation at the front.

Bumaru, like every other mission station in Biafra, became a vast refugee camp. The hospital overflowed and schooling was abandoned as all the nuns became fully occupied with the task of nursing. Malnutrition and Kwashiorkor made their appearance in the swollen bellies and stick limbs of the children, along with increasing levels of disease and the new horrors of shrapnel wounds, severed limbs and shattered bones. The girl child who had lost her home, her parents and her foot on that first dark night was the first of many, and they had called her Aliya.

Early in May Prescott sought out O'Keefe. The priest had worked tirelessly and during the past months had found only the minimum time to preach and pray. There had been no time at all to relax and indulge in any long after-dinner conversation, and some of the uncertain animosity that had existed between them had been bridged.

"I'm leaving," Prescott said calmly. "It's time to get out."

"Is the book finished?"

"It was finished weeks ago."

O'Keefe smiled faintly. Once he would have been glad to see the back of this man but now he was not so sure. "It could have been finished months ago, if you hadn't devoted so much of your time to helping out with our work. I'm grateful."

"I had to earn my keep." Prescott was almost embarrassed. "But I don't see any point in staying any longer. The war must end soon. Biafra is being strangled and can't possibly survive. The airport at Port Harcourt is the only way out so I'll leave while there's still a chance. The final phase could

119

be quite horrific." He paused. "Perhaps you should come with me, and Sister Bernadette, and Mary."

"I know that I can speak for Sister Bernadette. These are our people, and Bumaru is our home. We will remain."

Prescott nodded slowly. He had not expected any other answer. "You could persuade Mary."

"You are free to ask her — and she is free to go."

"I have asked her, and she won't go."

"Then there is nothing I can do." O'Keefe spread his hands and smiled again. All his movements were tired, and all his smiles were faint.

Prescott shrugged. Mary Kerrigan had been quite adamant in her decision to stay, and enlisting the aid of the priest had been one last try without any real hope. He recognized a lost battle and moved on.

"There's the problem of my Land Rover. I had intended to ship it out of Port Harcourt, but there'll be no sea passages now the port is under a Federal blockade. The best thing I can do is to give it to you. I'll drive it to the airport, and if you can spare Daniel for a day he can come with me and bring it back."

"We'll use it as long as the petrol lasts and then keep it safe until you can send for it or return," O'Keefe promised. He was thoughtful for a moment and then added. "But I have to make a trip into Port Harcourt. We're fast running out of food and medical supplies and I have to make a report to the Catholic Mission Office. I'll come with you instead of Daniel."

★ ★ ★

They left soon after daybreak the following morning, Prescott driving, Mary Kerrigan in the passenger seat beside him, and O'Keefe hunched in the back. The list of drugs and medical requirements which Mary carried was a long one and they knew from weary experience that most of them would not be available. Mary accompanied them because she was best fitted to select whatever alternatives they could find.

Prescott drove as hard as he dared. He knew O'Keefe was impatient to return to Bumaru as soon as possible. However, the roads were churned up by troop convoys and choked with military traffic and aimlessly wandering refugees. Those who had fled south from Nsukka and Enugu mingling helplessly with those who had fled north from Bonny and Port Harcourt. The whole Ibo nation, once one of the most prosperous, industrious and advanced peoples of West Africa, was being slowly crushed into poverty, death and despair. The corpses at the roadside, those who had limped or crawled until they died of starvation, war wounds or disease, evoked the least pity. It was the desperate living with pleading eyes and outstretched skeleton hands which they could only ignore who tore at their hearts.

Mary had become accustomed to suffering over the past few months. Once she would not have believed that she could bear to see so much, but there was a toughness beneath her gentle nature, a tenacity of spirit that enabled her to go on. She could not become hardened to suffering, but she could accept that it happened and continue her efforts to help. Now, outside Bumaru, the scale of suffering was too vast for her to offer any comfort, and suddenly she felt as helpless as the refugees themselves. There was a mist in her eyes and she wanted to weep.

Once she caught sight of O'Keefe in the rear-view mirror. The priest was slumped forward with his face buried in his huge hands. She saw a tear trickle through his fingers and run down the back of his wrist and knew that he was crying.

Prescott drove in silence with a grim face. None of them were in a mood to talk. They passed through Owerri, a town swollen to six or seven times its original population with dull-faced crowds and long food queues. Further south the road became less congested, a sign that offered more threat than promise. They passed burned-out trucks where the vultures were still gorging and Mary squeezed her eyes shut. Prescott steered the Land Rover around the bomb craters that scarred the road.

They reached Port Harcourt late in the afternoon and found a war-ravaged town occupied mainly by Biafran soldiers. The once-imposing Shell-BP building had been gutted by fire and they could hear artillery shells being fired from the swampy creeks to the south of the great oil refinery, the biggest in West Africa. The refinery was still intact, although flames and smoke mushroomed from the pipeline that had been blown up by the Biafrans to hold back the Federal advance from the sea.

Prescott eased up on the accelerator as they entered town and glanced back over his shoulder. "Where to now?" He asked O'Keefe.

"Marcus Street, number thirty-six. It's an old villa used for accommodation by the Mission Society. We can stay there overnight. You'll be welcome too, of course."

Prescott stared at him. O'Keefe was pale and his temples glistened with sweat. It was hot and stuffy inside the Land Rover despite the open windows, and Prescott could feel his own shirt sticking to his body. However, it was the first time he had noticed O'Keefe show any sign of being affected by the heat.

"Are you alright?" Prescott asked.

"It's been a tiring journey." O'Keefe's smile was strained.

Prescott nodded and turned back to the wheel. O'Keefe gave directions and Marcus Street was easy to find, it was a residential street of faded villas that now looked abandoned. The windows were all shuttered and the gardens overgrown and littered with rubbish. Prescott stopped the Land Rover outside number thirty-six and they all climbed out. Prescott stretched his shoulder muscles. Mary rubbed one hand over her aching eyes and felt sweat and dust under her fingertips. Behind them O'Keefe struggled to control an involuntary shiver before leading the way inside.

The villa was empty except for an African caretaker, an old man with grey wool hair and fearful eyes who came slowly after several minutes of knocking on the door. He recognized O'Keefe and let them in. They had come at a bad time, he informed them. Port Harcourt was braced for a Federal attack at any moment.

★ ★ ★

They left the villa as quickly as possible. In normal circumstances they would have bathed and then relaxed in their allotted rooms, but their business was urgent and the sense of impending disaster which overhung the hot, shuttered streets was very strong. Vultures soared in the distant sky, like impatient guests arrived too early for a banquet.

Prescott dropped Mary and O'Keefe at the Catholic Mission Office and then drove out to the airport. Twice he was stopped by Biafran roadblocks, bamboo poles supported on oil drums to span the road, and each time he had difficulty in arguing his way through. At the airport he found the Nigerian Airways office closed. The only flights in and out of Port Harcourt were the irregular Super Constellations flown via Portuguese Guinea and Sao Thome Island by a nameless charter firm based in Lisbon. The flights ferried in supplies and arms and Prescott spent a frustrating hour before finding an official who would admit to knowing any details of this clandestine operation. The man was a half caste with crinkled hair, thick lips and sallow skin. He was wary until

Prescott opened up his shirtfront and pulled his British passport and a book of British traveller's cheques from the body belt around his waist.

"The planes only land at night," the half caste told him. "You must appreciate it is dangerous. There is artillery fire. The planes need the cover of darkness. They return empty, so perhaps tonight you can get a seat to Sao Thome, or Lisbon. Or perhaps tomorrow night." He glanced greedily at the chequebook. "I can sell you a ticket now."

"Tonight," Prescott said. "When we're sure I can get on a plane."

"Be here at midnight. My name is Garcia — make sure you ask for me. But I cannot promise it will be tonight."

"I'll be here." Prescott zipped up his body belt and buttoned his shirt.

"Two hundred pounds," the half caste warned him. "It will cost at least two hundred pounds."

"To Sao Thome, or to Lisbon?"

"Just to get out." The half caste smiled. His teeth were the best feature in his face.

* * *

When he returned to the town Prescott stopped at the only hotel that was still open and ordered a beer in the deserted bar. He needed the drink to slake the dust from his throat and the taste was good. There had been no alcohol at Bumaru so it was an old acquaintance to be renewed. One of the credit points to the African climate, in Prescott's view, was that it made cold beer taste even better. He decided he could take a couple more and an hour passed before he climbed back into the Land Rover and headed for the villa. It was eight o'clock in the evening, the sun had gone down and the sultry air was even heavier with foreboding in the darkness. Every shadow was a menace and twice he heard bursts of machine gun fire in the distance. The soldiers were trigger-happy. Prescott planned a shower and three hours sleep before saying his goodbyes to Mary and O'Keefe, and then asking the priest to drive him out to the airport.

His plans came immediately unstuck, for he returned to find O'Keefe shivering violently under a great pile of blankets on one of the two single beds in the room they had been given to share. The priest was unconscious, his face drenched with cold sweat, the white hair wild and disarrayed and his teeth chattering noisily in a high fever. Mary stood over him and struggled to hold him down on the bed as he fought to twist and turn. She looked round wearily as Prescott came into the room, her face filled with sudden relief.

"Malaria," she explained briefly. "He knew it was coming on and tried to get the food supplies arranged before the attack started. One of the Fathers from the Mission Office helped me to get him back here."

O'Keefe kicked at his blankets and almost rolled off the bed. Mary moved quickly to stop him but then his arm jerked in a stiff flailing movement that almost swept her aside. Prescott added his weight to stop the sick man from tumbling to the floor and together they only just succeeded. O'Keefe was a heavy man and a fighter. When they had restrained him and he fell back Mary was panting. Her face was still dirty from the journey and Prescott realized that if she had not found the time to wash then neither would she have found the time to rest or eat. He thought of the hour he had spent over his beer and felt guilty.

"Take a break," he advised. "I'll watch over him for a while."

"Thanks, Geoff," Mary was too exhausted to argue. She stepped back from the bed and then hesitated before leaving the room. "Did you book a flight?"

Prescott thought of Garcia waiting for him at midnight. Obviously O'Keefe would not now be driving him out to the airport. He could perhaps take a taxi, or take the Land Rover and leave it there for O'Keefe to collect later. Or — He shut down on his thoughts because he knew he wouldn't be using any of those alternatives tonight.

"There's nothing for a couple of days," he said calmly.

Mary smiled and went out reassured.

Somewhere, muffled by the night, a machine gun stuttered, and the heavy 105 metre howitzers began pumping out the first of the nightly barrages of shells from behind the Federal battle lines in the swamps and jungles to the south.

★ ★ ★

It was a long, sleepless night for many people. Some stayed awake through fear, some through necessity, and some with a fierce, driving eagerness to see the new dawn. One of the latter was the officer commanding K Company of Federal Nigeria's Third Division Marine Commandos, Captain David Katsina. He bared his teeth in a tigerish smile each time the big guns roared and throughout the night he glanced frequently and impatiently at the heavy gold watch on his left wrist. He was tired of the swamps, the dripping curtains of the mangroves, the infuriating buzz of insects, and the mud which stained his once gloss-polished black boots. Also he was a Yoruba, a proud and haughty individual, one of the new ruling class with no love for the clannish Ibos. He itched to advance, to attack, to storm forward to victory on a wave of Ibo blood. And he had goaded his men with praise and curses into a similar lusting frenzy.

K Company was encamped on a spit of hard land between two creeks with their boats drawn up on either side, the same boats they had used to storm Bonny far too many months ago. Federal Nigeria had purchased or impounded every craft over eighteen

133

foot in length to launch the initial sea-borne invasion of Biafra, and K Company had been one of the first to hit the beaches. Katsina and his men had fought their way ashore to capture the vital oil installations, shooting down the Biafran defenders and driving those who survived back into the mangroves.

During that engagement Katsina had earned a reputation for leadership and toughness which many of his fellow company commanders already envied. He had the right background, he had received his military training at Sandhurst, and he was determined to carve a name for himself in this war. He was a short, stocky man, his black face handsome beneath his green helmet. He saw himself as dashing, confident and ruthless, and he lived up to his own image. At Bonny he had shown no mercy and he drilled his men in his own code.

Katsina knew that this was an era when military men ruled over

Africa, and education and an officer's commission were the twin keys to power. And power was his ultimate aim. Today he was only a captain, but the Federal army was expanding fast and promotion came even faster on the battlefield. Despite his hatred for the Ibos Katsina was almost grateful to them for this war. It was his opportunity. He had steeled himself to become the leader his men would follow into the jaws of death itself, the victor whom the press would glorify. Today it is General Gowon, he told himself often with his tiger smile, tomorrow it will be General Katsina.

Three hours before dawn the artillery fire intensified. The sound was thunderous music to Katsina's ears and his smile became a broad slash of white teeth in a face that was almost invisible in the gloom. He had become impatient with the long months of delay, making forays and fighting brief but bloody skirmishes in the swampy jungles between Bonny and Port Harcourt. He had fretted and cursed with frustration as the big howitzers were hauled up to the battle lines and the troops flowed in slowly behind him, but at last the hour of the final attack was near. While the big guns crashed he made the final rounds of his men, checking their packs, their weapons and the boats for the tenth time that night. He was a tireless man, always moving, never satisfied unless he was doing something. Now, instead of minutes, there were only seconds between the endless glances at the big gold watch on his wrist.

The radio messages began to crackle an hour before dawn, and the first was the command for K Company to advance. The commandos moved swiftly to their boats. Already the scouting parties had gone ahead in swift, silently paddled native canoes. Katsina leaped nimbly into the bows of a twenty foot motor cutter, the spearhead of his assorted fleet. A sergeant joined him, crouching behind the machine gun bolted down to the narrowing deckboards behind the bowsprit. A dozen commandos, bristling with sub-machine guns, automatic rifles and mortars, crowded into the cockpit behind the wheel cabin. The cutter sank dangerously low in the brackish water. Two of the biggest men wielded long bamboo poles and on Katsina's order the boat was pushed off from the sandspit. The rest of the fleet followed in single file.

Silently except for the steady drip and splash of the poles the long line of boats threaded its way along the winding creek between overhanging flanks of dank, black jungle. Wet leaves and dangling fronds of foliage slapped at Katsina's face and forced him to crouch down beside the sergeant. Mosquitos and sand flies swirled around their heads but were ignored. Katsina felt tension, elation, happiness and above all ambition struggling for supremacy within his breast. He welcomed the coming battle as another chance to step up through the ranks. He would emerge from the swamps a captain, but if the gods were willing he would enter Port Harcourt a major.

The darkness weakened. The first grey half light of dawn filtered through the mangroves. They moved through an eerie, nightmare world of black water, mudbanks and great clutching tangles of roots. Sodden greenery made a canopy over their heads. Katsina stared ahead, straining his eyes through the gloom. He saw the ugly, bulbous eyes of a crocodile, and then the narrow thrust of a canoe darting back to meet them.

The canoe scout made a brief report. Two hundred yards ahead the creek emerged from the jungle. There on either side were machine gun nests, each one manned by three Biafran soldiers. Katsina called up the two boats behind and disembarked six men on to each bank under the command of two of his sergeants. He gave them their orders and watched them claw their way out of sight over the mud and mangrove roots.

He waited twenty minutes, listening to the fury of the big guns which were hurling shells high over their heads at the enemy. The sound was a world apart, sometimes strangely remote from the hushed silence here at swamp level. Then he heard the stutter of automatic fire and the crack of a grenade explosion further down the creek. He shouted an order and every boatman started his engine, some of them roaring swiftly and violently into life, others spluttering and coughing to the accompaniment of kicks and curses.

Katsina lost no more time. He yelled at his pilot and the cutter charged forward. He drew his revolver and the sergeant crouched more tensely over the machine gun. He didn't look back to see how many boats were following. The roar of engines told him he was not alone and the slow boats could catch up later. They sped through the green tunnel with the boats behind bucking violently, almost uncontrollably in their churned wake. Seconds later the cutter was shooting out of the mangrove curtain and into open reeds and grassland.

One machine gun nest was silent, but the other on the left bank was still operational. Its fire was directed at the prone bodies of the advance party of commandos and before the Biafrans could swing the hot muzzle round the cutter was upon them. The sergeant blazed away and Katsina fired his revolver over the flashing muzzle of their machine gun. The Biafrans slumped dead over their weapon and the boats surged on.

After fifty yards they came under more enemy sniper fire. The sergeant was flung away from the machine gun and Katsina saw blood on his screaming black face as he rolled off the bows and into the creek. He vanished and Katsina crouched in his place, not caring whether the man was alive or dead. There was no time to turn back.

He raked the bank ahead with bullets, glorifying in the stink of cordite and the hammering of the stock against his shoulder. Then the cutter's bows ploughed into the bank where the river made a bend and the belt feed into the machine gun jammed.

Cursing Katsina scrambled ashore. They were getting a hot reception now and there was no choice but to abandon the boats. His men followed his example, throwing themselves full length in the grass. One of them died at Katsina's side and he shoved his revolver back into its holster and took up the dead man's sub-machine gun.

On the skyline he could see the black smoke of fresh oil fires, and over Port Harcourt itself lay the black pall of more burning. The big guns were still pounding away at the airport runway, and all along the jungle line the commandos of the Third Division were emerging and pushing their remorseless way forward. Katsina hurled abuse and exhortation at his men and led their advance, wriggling swiftly through the long grass on his elbows and belly with his sub-machine gun ready to fire. He was eager to meet the enemy, and anxious to be the first Federal officer to enter Port Harcourt.

★ ★ ★

Prescott was well aware that a major battle was taking place, but he had no time to spare any thought for its implications. All through the night he was occupied with the task of restraining O'Keefe who was alternately sweating and shivering in fits of violent convulsions. Racked by fever the priest was still a powerful man and alone Mary would never have managed to control him. Both of them were weary by dawn when O'Keefe finally relapsed into a drained and fitful sleep.

For the last hour the guns had kept up a continuous barrage and several times the shells had fallen close enough to shake the villa. Another impact sounded close by and they felt the blast through the walls and floors. Chunks of plaster fell from the cracking ceiling and the light bulb performed a puppet's dance on its flex. Mary trembled and looked at Prescott. Her eyes were full of unspoken questions.

Prescott moved over to the window and lifted up the slatted blind to look down into the street. He saw an ambulance go past and a dozen soldiers moving hurriedly and glancing back over their shoulders. They wore the bright rising sun shoulder flashes of the Biafran army, but they had a beaten and dejected look. Their uniforms were soiled with mud and two of them wore tatters of blood bandages. Prescott could hear the crack of mortars and long bursts of automatic small arms fire above the boom of the big howitzers. He turned back to Mary.

"The Biafrans are on the run. The Federal army must be hot on their heels. We have to get out of here."

She looked doubtfully at O'Keefe. "He needs care and rest."

"He won't get it here. Stay with him while I find the caretaker."

Mary nodded and Prescott left her. He searched the ground floor of the villa, calling to the grey-haired African to come out of hiding, but it was all in vain. He returned to the bedroom and shrugged his shoulders.

"The old man's bolted — can't say that I blame him. We'll have to get the good Father down to the Land Rover without his help."

Mary was sitting on the second bed with her shoulders slumped, but she hadn't forgotten why they were here. She looked up slowly. "Geoff, we can't go straight back to Bumaru. We have to load up the food and medical supplies. They should be ready and waiting at the Mission Office."

Prescott hesitated. The sound of small arms fire was ominously close and his impulse was to get away as quickly as possible. Then he thought of the sick and hungry faces at Bumaru.

"Alright, wait here while I pick them up."

"It's best if I go. They know me."

"Don't argue." Prescott pushed her down firmly as she started to get up. "You're not going out on the streets alone."

She stared at him, her eyes red-rimmed and her face white and strained. He forced her a smile.

"I'll be back within an hour. Stay in the villa and keep quiet. You should be alright."

She nodded slowly and he hurried out to the Land Rover.

He drove quickly to the Mission Office through streets that swarmed with soldiers. The Biafrans were in retreat but fighting a bitter rearguard action. Smoke clouds rolled over the city where some of the big stores and office blocks were being gutted by fire. Disorder and confusion reigned everywhere and he guessed that the troops who blocked his way now had withdrawn from the contested battleground to the south. Shells were still falling heavily in the direction of the airport and he thought briefly and bitterly of that last severed link with the outside world.

★ ★ ★

After Prescott had gone Mary checked that O'Keefe was still sleeping quietly and then went to her own room. She stripped and took a shower before putting on fresh underwear and relaxing thankfully on the bed. She closed her eyes, intending to rest them for a few moments only, but almost immediately she fell asleep.

She came awake reluctantly to the tinkle of broken glass, a sound which penetrated slowly into her dulled mind. She opened her eyes and remembered O'Keefe with a sudden feeling of guilt. She had left the doors open so she would hear if he stirred and he was her first thought. Quickly she swung to her feet and moved out on to the landing to glance into his room.

The priest lay quiet beneath his blankets, his breathing deep and even. Mary stared uncertainly and then a door banged below. She realized that she had not heard the sound of the Land Rover and it was too soon for Prescott to have returned. Suddenly she was scared.

Her first instinct to was bolt back into her room and get fully dressed, but even as it arrived the impulse was too late. A door opened below and a strange African appeared in the small hallway at the foot of the staircase. He was a soldier, although from which army she could not determine. He carried a rifle and wore army boots and uniform trousers. His upper torso was bare, streaked with sweat and dirt. His step was furtive, his head twisting left and right, and then he looked up.

They stared at each other, and in that moment they were both afraid.

The African was not alone. Mary could hear more movements and voices in the kitchen. She guessed they were men who had deserted or separated from their unit and were now taking advantage of the confusion and panic to indulge in a private spree of looting. Her heart hammered and her legs felt weak as she struggled to control her fear.

"This house is not abandoned," she said as firmly as she was able. "Please go away before I call the police."

The man was startled by her presence but still he did not move. There was a shocked hush and then two more Africans appeared, their youthful faces were startled and their arms were filled with food from the refrigerator.

As the three pairs of eyes gawked at her up the staircase Mary became acutely aware of her own body. She wore only her bra and panties and felt as though even they had been peeled away to leave her naked.

"Go away!" she shouted, but her fear

had returned and was reflected in her voice.

By now they had sensed that she was alone and offered them no danger. Slowly and horribly the bare-chested man with the rifle smiled.

Mary's nerve broke and she fled back to her room. She slammed the door behind her and turned to search frantically for a key or a bolt. There was neither. Panic gripped her and she grabbed for her clothes which lay across the foot of the bed. She succeeded in pulling on her skirt but before she could zip it up the door had opened and the three African soldiers stood watching her. Their hands were empty, all ready to reach out and touch her, and all three were grinning.

Mary screamed.

The scream was like a spur. The bare-chested man spoke hoarsely to his companions, his words thick with excitement, and then they rushed into the room. There was nowhere for Mary to run and within seconds their hands were all over her, pulling at her clothes, groping for the intimate parts of her body and struggling to smother her cries.

She fell backwards on to the bed with the three Africans fighting to get on top of her, and terror gripped her heart as the hastily donned skirt was ripped away. For a few moments it was entangled around her thrashing legs and then with another violent tear it was free. Mary sank her teeth into the hand that sought to cover her mouth and shrieked hysterically as it was pulled away. Then her shoulders were pinned to the bed and the bare-chested man was shouting at his friends to hold her still as he forced his way between her legs. With one hand he was trying to claw down the flimsy material of her panties and with the other he was feverishly pulling open his own trousers.

Mary was ready to faint. Her screams had blotted out the sound of the returning Land Rover and for a moment the white hand clamping down on the sweating shoulder of the black man looming over her was just one more unreality in the whole agonizing nightmare. Then Prescott hauled the negro back, spun him round and smashed an angry fist into the thick-lipped, lust-filled face.

Prescott had arrived at a run and maintained his momentum. As the African reeled away to crash against the wall Prescott followed him up with two more savage blows. The African lurched against the open window and Prescott helped him through with a well-aimed kick to the groin. The man fell backwards to the garden below with a sharp screech that ended as abruptly as it had begun.

Prescott turned to face the two youths. The bravest was already leaping for his back and Prescott sliced him across the throat with the edge of his left hand, again using the whole swing of his body to add power to the blow. The boy went down like a sapling chopped in its prime by a woodman's axe.

The third African was still gaping with amazement and when he moved it was to flee. Prescott was breathing heavily and allowed him to escape. It was many years since he had last indulged in such violent exercise and he was badly out of training. Enough was enough.

After a moment he dragged the fallen youth across the floor and out on to the landing. He returned and closed the door behind him. He glanced through the window to see the man he had pitched out crawling in painful retreat across the grass below. Finally he turned to Mary.

She was standing, facing him, white-faced and still trembling. She had a very lovely body and the fact strangely disturbed and surprised him. Too lovely to mask in the sexless white coat she usually wore, he thought briefly. He moved to pick up her skirt from the floor and offered it to her. He was faintly embarrassed and for once he was at a loss for something adequate to say.

Mary barely saw the offered skirt. She went to meet him, faltered, and then wrapped her arms around his waist. Her legs were reluctant to support her and she needed his chest to lean on. Prescott held her until her trembling stopped, talking vague words of comfort which she did not hear. She was listening to the quickened beating of his heart.

Slowly Mary remembered again that she was all but naked, but now it did not seem to matter. After what he had already witnessed she had no more shame. Her emotions were suddenly confused and as she pressed against him her loins seemed to melt. The thought of what had nearly happened to her had roused a whole sea of natural feelings and desires which had been left dormant by her self-imposed isolation at the mission. It was a long time since her body had known the joy of sexual union with a man, and what had been attempted so crudely by the three soldiers would not be nearly so terrible if performed with some tenderness by Prescott. Abruptly she was trembling once more at the thought.

Prescott sensed her change of mood, and felt his own body begin to respond. He stared down into her wide searching eyes and understood. His hands began to caress her bare shoulders. The skin texture of his palms was rough, but his touch was sure and gentle.

"Geoff," she whispered, and then her thoughts somersaulted in a sudden rush of doubt.

"Mary," he answered huskily, with a sense of guilt. At the mission he had regarded her as being on par with the nuns.

He would have kissed her then but the moment was destroyed. In the next room O'Keefe groaned in his fevered sleep, and seconds later a shell exploded close enough to rock the building with its blast.

"We have to get out," Prescott said with regret. With Port Harcourt on the point of capture there was no time for anything else.

7

MAXWELL pulled the Delfin L 29 out of yet another dawn bombing run and looked back on the now familiar pattern of burning huts and vehicles. At this stage he had lost count of exactly how many missions he had flown, and with every power station and similar standing military target in Biafra bombed out the raids on troop camps and concentrations had become stereotyped routine. Below there would be frenzied screaming and the harsh crackle of flames, but climbing back up to ten thousand feet it was a remote film without sound. Smoke clouds rolled over the jungle clearing, a discreet blanket for the dead and dying, and then it was all hidden from view.

"One more for the record," Tucker said, unemotional and pausing only briefly as he chewed the inevitable caramel.

Maxwell nodded but didn't speak. He had a dull headache, a pressing heaviness over his eyes which threatened to become permanent. He had buried his conscience with Lou Hendrix but there was still no job satisfaction in what they were doing. The civil war at ground level was ugly, involved and seemingly endless, leaving no more room for the naive belief that their presence could help it to a speedy and decisive conclusion. Lately Maxwell had begun to drink more heavily and there was still a sour taste in his mouth from the previous night. Whisky pilots was the current Nigerian term for most of the white mercenary flyers, and Maxwell knew he was becoming no better than the rest.

Tucker knew too and had told him to cool it. If the job was too dirty it was time to get out. Their combined bank balances were building up handsomely and Maxwell was almost ready to take

Tucker's advice — before it got to the point where he was drinking more than they were earning.

They were alone in the sky. Since Hendrix had died Maxwell preferred it that way. He was still opposed to the indiscriminate bombing of civilian targets, which set him and Tucker in a class of their own. They both knew that if they hadn't hit hard and consistently at the targets that mattered then they would have been dismissed months ago.

"Home," Maxwell said. He banked the plane to port, headed north and relaxed. He anticipated a trouble-free return flight because so far every flight had been smooth and easy. As he had predicted there had been no mid-air dog fights between the mercenary pilots of either side, and although Biafran ground fire could get hot and furious most of it was badly aimed.

What he didn't know was that the ever-busy arms salesmen who had flocked to reap the golden harvest of war had pulled off another big sale. Biafra had recently installed a battery of six radar-controlled Bofors anti-aircraft guns at a cost of eighty thousand dollars each; plus a number of ground-to-air heat-seeking missiles.

He found out as he re-crossed the battle lines at twenty thousand feet. The impact came without warning as though they had run into an invisible brick wall and the aircraft was slammed cartwheeling across the sky.

Pain tore through Maxwell's left leg, the air was crashed from his chest and his head felt as though it had been ripped off. He heard Tucker's scream, harsh and highpitched, the echoes drilling in his ears long after the original sound had stopped. The Delfin's nose had kicked up as it looped the loop and now it was falling and spinning through the sky. Maxwell was thrown forward again over the controls and his straps were tearing him apart. His teeth had split the inside of his lip and blood filled his mouth. The cotton wool clouds and the green jungle horizon were revolving crazily around the cockpit and he felt sick from the centrifugal force churning in his gut. He wanted to throw up.

He was blind, dazed and virtually helpless, but one desperately functioning corner of his brain was still sending command signals to his hands. Instinctively he pulled back on the control column and held it there with all his weight. The Delfin continued her spiralling dive, but slowly it became less steep. Impact was only seconds away with the jungle tree-tops almost within touching distance when the screaming aircraft levelled out. In the same moment a barrage of machine-gun ground fire shredded the wings and fuselage with bullet holes.

Jagged stars were punched through the toughened perspex of the cockpit and the altimeter and speed gauge dials on his control panel shattered before his eyes, but miraculously Maxwell escaped another personal hit. He hauled the staggering fighter into a climb and regained height, a mere two-thousand feet before the plane refused to obey any further and lurched sideways into another sliding dive.

Despite his shock and confusion Maxwell was aware that the rising white fireball of the sun was now dazzling off his port wing. The sun should have been to starboard and the fact that its position had reversed told him that somehow he had turned a complete circle and was heading back over the hostile heartland of Biafra. He tried to bring the plane round but the slack movement of the stick gave him no real control. He felt sick again and there was a warm, wet wave flowing over his thigh, seeping down his leg and slowly filling his leather flying boot.

"Brad," he spoke hoarsely but there was no answer.

"Brad?" he cried again, but all he could hear was the sudden, ominous crackle of flames and a dull roaring to his right.

He twisted his head and saw his starboard wing trailing a streamer of black smoke and tongues of red fire.

His instinct was to eject, but Tucker could still be alive — unconscious but alive. Silence did not necessarily mean death. He tried to shift in his seat and look over his shoulder, but pain wrenched at his ribs and Tucker was slumped below his line of vision. Cursing and sobbing he turned back to his losing battle at the controls.

There was only a minimum of response from the stick but he struggled to hold her up for as long as possible. His stunned senses were still in a whirl but the blazing wing was going to break off at any moment and he had only seconds to make a decision. Eject or crash were his only alternatives, but he couldn't bring himself to abandon Tucker.

Then he saw the ribbon of grey through the green.

The rain forest was sliced up by an irregular maze of rivers, some large, some small, all draining into the vast delta of the Niger, the swamps and the sea. This was one of the wider tributaries and with more fear than hope Maxwell banked the falling aircraft towards it. Sweat poured out of him as he wrestled violently with the sloppy control column. The green horizon tilted up to meet his port wing, steadied, and then dropped away again. Maxwell jerked more fiercely at the stick. The horizon came up again and the nose came round. It was enough to bring the plane on course with the flow of the river below. Maxwell pushed the stick to put her nose down and dropped his flaps and wheels to cut his airspeed. The grey ribbon of water rushed up to meet him.

The crash landing was going to kill them, he was sure of that. The river was too narrow and contorted. The rain forest crowded too close upon its banks. As an emergency runway it was a disaster but there was nothing else. The plane couldn't stay airborne and if it smashed into the forest it would disintegrate. Maxwell didn't expect that God would be listening, but he prayed. It was too late now to eject.

The trees flashed past beyond his wingtips. The river was coming up too fast and he strained back on the stick. There was a bone-jarring crash as his wheels hit down on the surface of the water and he was hurled forward against his harness. The Delfin's wings decapitated a great swathe of trees on either bank and then the blazing starboard wing snapped off with a terrible wrenching crack and exploded behind him. The long silver fuselage careered on, ploughing deeper and throwing up huge waves of spray. Maxwell screamed in a white-hot surge of undefined agony and blacked out. The Delfin hurtled forward for another hundred yards with the remaining wing scything through the trees. The drag of the river reduced its headlong speed and then it hit a sandbank and crashed to a dead stop. The tail reared up as the fuselage swivelled round behind a gigantic rising curtain of tumbled water, and then both the fuselage and the port wing finally cracked in two with almost simultaneous reports like the double bang of two massive howitzer guns exploding in unison.

The Delfin's nose began to sink slowly and the up-tilted stub of the broken wing burst into flames.

★ ★ ★

There was roaring and gurgling, the two sounds competing for supremacy, and a cold wetness climbing up his knees, embracing his thighs and buttocks. The sensations overcame the pain and darkness and Maxwell realized that he was conscious again. The roaring was the fire just beyond the cockpit to his left, the gurgling the inrush of the river as it forced its way inside the fuselage. Maxwell wanted to retreat into the merciful darkness, away from the pain, but then he thought of Tucker.

He made the effort to grope for the quick-release catches of his harness and the straps fell loose. He struggled free and pushed open the cockpit hood.

Heat from the fire singed his face. Smoke and fumes struck at his throat and nostrils, mixed with the taste of blood and set him choking. He twisted and hauled himself on to his knees, crouching in his seat and staring back at Tucker. One glance was enough to convince him that Brad was dead. Tucker was slumped and bloodied with his head lolling to one side and a gaping red wound showing across his neck beneath the hard edge of his flying helmet. The top of his spinal column had been violently severed.

Maxwell collapsed into more pain as his left leg crumpled beneath him. He almost passed out from the double nausea brought on by his mental and physical agonies. Suddenly he wanted to get away from the horror of his friend's death and the impulse combined with the failing instinct to

166

survive. He got both arms over the edge of the open cockpit and dragged himself out. For a second he sprawled poised over the sinking nose of the plane, his leg dangled uselessly behind him. Heat blistered his face and the sleeve of his flying jacket smouldered and leaped into flame. He was spent, but the Delfin suddenly tilted and settled deeper into the river. The movement sent him slithering forward over the curve of the fuselage and then the swirl of muddy waters engulfed him.

The shock brought him back from the edge of unconsciousness and he struggled feebly. Water forced its way into his nose and mouth and instead of burning alive he was drowning. The flow of the river carried him fifty yards and then it made a bend. Suddenly it was shallow and he clawed at the sandy bottom with his hands. He crawled out coughing and gasping, using two hands and one knee. His left leg still trailed in the river. Pain washed over him again as he emerged and he lay face-down and helpless on the river's edge.

Behind him the fuel tanks exploded with a mighty roar, showering blazing fragments of wreckage over the entire area. Those which landed in the river were extinguished in great hissing gouts of steam, while others started minor fires along the wake of mutilated foliage which lined both banks.

Maxwell made the effort to lift his face from the mud and stared back at the furiously burning wreckage. The once-proud jet fighter had become Tucker's funeral pyre and he groaned and wept with anguish.

★ ★ ★

Five minutes passed before he began to take stock of his situation and realized that the mere act of being alive had left him with the problem of staying alive. When he was capable of thinking it was obvious that the pillar of black smoke from the plane crash would soon attract visitors, and it was equally obvious they

168

would not be of a friendly disposition. Any Biafran troops who found him would be more likely to finish him off on the spot, in the most agonizing manner they could devize.

It was difficult to assess the full scope of his injuries. He knew he had a shattered leg and the rest of his body seemed to be bruised, battered and bloodied on every limb. However, he tried to crawl, and although it proved a slow and excruciating process he found that he was capable of movement. He dragged himself out of the river and into the jungle.

He was not a moment too soon, for almost immediately he heard the sound of approaching vehicles. There were at least two trucks but he couldn't see them. They stopped some distance away and then he heard the excited sound of African voices. A minute passed while he lay trembling and then he saw the long grasses and bamboos part on the opposite bank. An Ibo soldier stepped warily through the gap

169

with a light machine gun cradled in his arms. His black face was solemn as he stared at the crashed fighter. Then his eyes began to roam slowly along both banks of the river.

Maxwell pressed himself deeper into the black hollow he had found beneath a green fringe of undergrowth and there he froze into stillness. He heard more soldiers arrive and the quick jabber of their voices. The voices separated and he knew they were searching along the far bank. He squeezed his eyes shut and gritted his teeth to suppress a whimper. He could only hope that they didn't really expect to find anyone alive, and that they wouldn't bother to cross the river.

He could hear the dying growl of the flames, and the hiss of steam as the Delfin subsided a few inches deeper into the mud. The voices continued, shouting at each other, and accompanied by the swish of branches and foliage being parted by booted feet and swinging rifle butts. For a moment the sounds were directly opposite and panic sent his heart pounding and dried up his mouth. He was sure there must be visible signs where he had crawled out of the river. Then the voices moved away, searching upstream.

Maxwell sighed with relief and opened his eyes. He eased his head out from his refuge and quickly scanned the far bank. There were no soldiers in sight and he decided that it would be pointless to wait and find out whether they did intend to cross the river. There was no future here, and the only alternative was to start moving.

He backed away from the river, levering himself with the palms of his hands, his right heel and buttock. His left trouser leg was a gory mess of blood and river water, but mercifully the leg itself had become partially numb. Only when it snagged on a root or grass tuft did he experience a knife stab of pain, and now he was more aware of the general mass of lesser hurts.

After a few minutes he decided that

moving backwards was not such a good idea, he was bumping blindly into too many obstacles. He paused to rest and then turned carefully on to his right side, facing forward. He was surrounded by tangled curtains of green but there were gaps where he could pull himself through. He dragged himself another hundred yards and then stopped to listen. He had left the river and the Ibo voices behind. He was alone in the jungle.

It was time to make a fresh analysis of his position. For the moment he had eluded capture but he was still in hostile country miles behind the Federal battle lines. The few bars of slanted light which penetrated through to the forest floor gave him a general idea of direction, and the only course he saw open was to keep crawling north until he was clear of Biafra. He didn't know how far he could travel or how long he could hope to stay alive, but it was the only alternative to giving up and dying where he lay.

Throughout the day he made slow, painful progress, dragging himself a few inches at a time, resting, and then dragging again. He sweated through dank, steamy thickets with the hot stench of rot and leaf mould cloying in his nostrils. He cursed his way through knotted nightmares of ferns, undergrowth and coarse grasses that scratched and whipped at his face and hands. He sobbed with frustration when the barriers of bush and jungle became too dense to penetrate and he was forced to make detours. Time after time he lay panting with exhaustion, waiting for his strength to build up and the pain waves to subside.

The Colt 0.45 he wore in a holster at his hip snagged repeatedly on the passing branches and several times he was tempted to throw it away. He had forgotten it in the moments when he might have needed it, while he cowered hidden from the searching soldiers, and now it seemed an unnecessary burden. At the same time he would be defenceless without it and he was still a long way from safety. He compromised by tugging it round to his belly where it lay more comfortably and snagged less often.

At midday when the sun was high he rested for an hour. His senses slipped away and a black veil descended. When it lifted again he was suffering from a terrible thirst and his lip had swollen like a bloated sausage. He raised himself on one elbow and was frightened by the effort it required. He looked down at the mud and dirt, which with the dried blood now encrusted his clothes and wounds, and shuddered at the thought of all the infection he had probably collected.

He began to move again, feebly. He was very weak now and it took twice as long and twice as much effort to make each dragging motion with his arms and shoulders. He persisted although he knew it was hopeless. The sun was hot as it moved through the afternoon sky and the sweat dripped steadily from his face. After another hour he realized that he was bleeding again and leaving a smeared red trail on the broken grass behind him.

By late afternoon there was no more doubt in his mind. He knew that never in a million years could he crawl all the way back to the Federal battle lines. In his present state he would not even survive the night. The shadows were lengthening into dusk and he was dying with the day. He thought of Brad, and of Claire, and he was not even sorry. He looked up to the sky and saw the wooden cross of Christ standing tall above the barrier of green bush, and despite the swollen lip he smiled.

He didn't ask himself how the cross came to be floating in the African sky. He didn't care if it was a mirage or a figment of his imagination. It was a new goal, a supremely more realistic goal than the vaguely defined limits of Federal territory. He set a new course and inched his way towards it. His brain swam in a sea of delusion but the cross remained. His eyes were closed and he felt terribly tired.

When he opened his eyes again for one last, brief glimpse of the cross it had miraculously shrunk to a six-inch crucifix dangling before his bewildered eyes on a silver chain. Behind the crucifix was the face of a woman framed in the white cowl of a nun. The face was white, kindly but uncertain. It was the face of a mother, or an angel. Angels were supposed to have wings and harps, but he decided that the nun's habit was not wholly out of context. He smiled at her and then fainted away into the waiting darkness.

Sister Bernadette knelt over him for a moment. Then she straightened up, gathered her black skirts and hurried to fetch help to carry him back to the mission.

8

THE days passed. O'Keefe recovered his strength. Maxwell began to heal. Prescott stayed. As the war continued millions of refugees streamed into the shrinking heartland of Biafra. Food and medical supplies dwindled rapidly and rations were cut to the minimum, halved, and then halved again. Each day the food queues grew longer, the faces more emaciated, the bodies more skeletal. There was no child without the grotesquely swollen belly that was the symbol of kwashiorkor, and no adult without dulled eyes sunk in despair.

Inevitably there were frequent quarrels among the refugees, and one of the worst occurred when a small python was spotted on the edge of the compound. Half a dozen men swiftly attacked it with sticks, battering the snake into the dust before its head was sliced off by the razor-edged swing of a heavy machete. Snake meat was edible and immediately the dispute began over who had earned the major share. Within seconds tempers flared and the men came to blows.

O'Keefe arrived at a run, the skirts of his robe flapping behind him like the wings of some great black, avenging eagle. The women's quarrels he wisely left alone, but savage fighting between men could result in death or injury and without hesitation he plunged into the middle of the struggling group. He towered over them and roared commands for them to stop, at the same time using his great strength to hurl them apart as though they were mere children.

Most of the Africans were shamed, backing away with downcast faces. The man with the machete had been thrown aside and landed on his hands and knees in the dust. He scrambled up to find that the priest had turned his back to admonish the rest of the group and there was red fury in his eyes. He raised the machete for an enraged blow which would have slain the priest as surely as it had decapitated the python.

Prescott reached the scene in the same second. His left hand flashed out to check the black wrist wielding the machete while his right fist dealt an abrupt, crippling punch to the African's kidneys. The machete and the man fell separately to the ground.

O'Keefe looked round, more surprised than shaken. It had never occurred to him that anyone would try to kill him.

"Thank you, Geoffrey," he said slowly. "But I hope you haven't hurt him."

"He'll recover." Prescott smiled briefly.

O'Keefe nodded, then moved to help the man up and hand him over to his fellows. He picked up the machete and made a quick count of the men involved, then he chopped the body of the python into six equal portions.

Afterwards he returned the big knife by its handle to the owner.

"One piece each," he said severely. "It's the only fair way."

The African looked sullen and was still rubbing his sore belly with one hand, but the hot flood of his rage had abated. O'Keefe turned and walked away, and after a moment Prescott followed.

* * *

The fleeing Ibos who escaped from the outer regions of Biafra, which were now occupied by the victorious Federal troops, brought with them a multitude of horror stories. They told of villages burned, women raped, the men herded together and butchered by machine guns. The more grisly tales spoke of ritual mutilations, and babies spitted like ripe melons on spears and knives. With these common memories and future fears, on top of the great physical wrench of being torn from their homes, and the emotional anguish of seeing so many of their friends and relatives dead, maimed or missing, the refugees suffered inevitably from a traumatic, soul-shattering upheaval of the spirit.

The tribe was decimated, the land ravaged by total war, the Gods had deserted them and even the graves of their ancestors had been left behind. Some sank into utter dejection and despair. Others looked up to the great wooden cross above the mission and prayed to Jesus. Others made offerings to the old Gods of their fathers, to the hierarchy of fetish spirits who lived in the trees and the earth and the wind, and who would intervene on their behalf with Chuku, the Supreme God of the Ibos. The prudent prayed to Jesus and made offerings through the spirit messengers to Chuku. In a time of national disaster it was impossible to know which God they had offended, or which God might still be capable of protecting His own.

It was Ruth Ekwensi who noticed that Daniel had taken to wearing his shirt buttoned up tight to the neck. She watched him return with Isaac and Alif from the dusty track that led past the mud huts of the village and through the bush to the river. Between them the three boys carried two full water cans, but where once they would have been smiling and laughing they were now silent and weary. They had to make the trip too often now for there to be any pleasure left in the excursion. Also they were all getting thinner, and less strong, no one was sleek and well fed any more.

They carried the cans on to the hospital verandah and stood them against the wall in the shade. Isaac and Alif sat down on the boards with their backs to the wall and closed their eyes. Daniel went inside and returned a few seconds later with the bottle of chloride pills that would make the water drinkable. He dropped a few tablets inside each can and took the bottle back.

When he emerged for the second time Sister Ruth called to him from the garden where she stood in the shade of the church.

"Daniel, come here a moment, please."

Daniel looked to the sound of her voice and hesitated. He was tired and he wanted to sit down with his friends. Isaac opened one eye and looked at him but said nothing. Reluctantly Daniel stepped down from the verandah and walked slowly through the hot sunlight to the garden.

The African nun watched him approach with some trepidation. She was almost certain of what she was going to find, although she prayed that she would be proved wrong.

"Daniel," her voice trembled. "What are you hiding under your shirt?"

Daniel looked guilty. His hand moved up, nearly touching the lowest shirt button before he checked it.

He let the hand fall back to his side.

"Nothing," he said hoarsely. He wished that his mouth was not so dry.

"Daniel," she was pained. "Hasn't Father O'Keefe taught us always to tell the truth?"

Daniel bit his lip and bowed his head. After a moment he nodded.

"Then show me, please. You are wearing something around your neck."

The boy was embarrassed. He clenched his fists for a moment and was tempted to refuse. A black devil was inside him but the habit of obedience was stronger. Slowly he opened the neck of his shirt, and without looking up he slipped the loop of string with its small, dangling leather bag over his head. He held it forward, still without raising his eyes.

Sister Ruth took it from his hand. Her own hand was trembling. She tugged at the draw-string with fumbling fingers and the neck of the amulet bag came open. She tipped out the contents into the palm of her hand, a three-inch crocodile tooth, yellow with age and wrapped in a torn-out page of close printed text.

"It is a very powerful fetish." Daniel was staring at her with wide, hopeful eyes. His words were rapid and intense. "The spirits of our ancestors lived in crocodiles, so this will protect me and keep the Hausa and Yoruba soldiers away from Bumaru."

"It will not protect you." The nun had tears in her eyes. "Only the love of Jesus can protect you. And what is this?" There was more shock in her voice as she spread out the folded paper, and recognized a page torn from the New Testament.

"The Bible is also a powerful fetish." Daniel said weakly.

Sister Ruth thrust the tooth and the paper back into the bag and thrust it into his hands.

"Throw it away," she ordered. "Throw

185

it as far as you can, and then go into the church and pray to Jesus for forgiveness from your sins. You know it is wrong to believe in a fetish. And you know it is wrong to tear pages from a Bible."

Daniel stared at her, angry and afraid, his chest a turmoil of mixed emotions. She looked fierce enough to beat him, and because Ruth Ekwensi was normally a kind and gentle young woman the transformation was doubly disturbing. Finally Daniel turned and threw the amulet bag away.

"Now go into the church," she scolded him. She miscalculated the twisted expression on his face and decided he had been suitably chastised. "I won't tell anyone," she promised him. "I'm sure you won't do it again."

Daniel nodded and fled into the church. There he prayed desperately to Jesus, hoping for a greater understanding of his terrible spiritual dilemma.

Later, when it was dark, he returned

to the garden. He had marked the spot where the amulet bag had fallen and after a hurried search he retrieved it. This time he pushed it deep into the pocket of his shorts where he hoped it would escape notice.

* * *

Even though Daniel's lapse from faith was kept from him, the revival of the old African beliefs could not escape O'Keefe's notice. He was aware of the upsurge of fetish worship, and the ugly rumours of witchcraft which circulated among his grossly swollen flock. It was murmured that a pregnant woman had given birth to twins, and that both babies had been immediately killed. Only one could have had a natural father, the other must have been planted in the mother's womb by an evil spirit, and how could anyone know which was which. Despair turned distraught minds on to old, dark paths, some of them almost forgotten, and at night the drums beat in the village as the mediums worked themselves into a trance or frenzy.

O'Keefe was worn out at the end of the day, but in an effort to check the spiritual degeneration around him he began to hold additional evening services in the mission church. The services were well attended, on every occasion the church was full with extra faces crowding at the windows and doors. Once the African congregation would have sung with joyful enthusiasm, but now the hymns were shouted with voices that were hollow, or filled with an urgent desperation. O'Keefe read his specially prepared sermons in tones of fire and thunder fit to terrify Satan himself, but still the drums throbbed and the rumours continued.

O'Keefe had the physical and moral courage to match his massive frame, and finally he made irregular patrols round the village and the dark fringes of bush and jungle surrounding the mission buildings and the compound. He broke up dances simply by revealing his presence. The drumming and then the dancing would stop as he approached, his mane of white hair a clear identification above his white collar and black robe, and then both musicians and dancers would pick up their instruments and melt swiftly away into the night. There were smaller, more private and sinister groups, who would somehow become alert and disappear before he could determine what they were doing.

He prowled about the village one night when the drums were silent. It was pitch black except for brief flares of firelight. There were no stars and no moon. Neither were there any dogs to betray him with their barking, for the dogs had all been eaten by the hungry Africans months before. He had borrowed a black scarf from Mary Kerrigan to hide his distinctive head, and this time he was able to get close to a furtive group who clustered around the doorway to one of the thatched bee-hive huts.

A shout of alarm went up when he was recognized and the Africans bolted. O'Keefe did not attempt to stop those who were already running but moved quickly forward to block the escape of those who were still trapped inside the hut. He ducked his head to enter the doorway and stared down at the circle of upraised black faces with wide, startled eyes. Smoke stung his throat and eyes from the small fire that threw a flickering light over the scene, and what he saw in the centre of the squatting circle filled him with disgust.

★ ★ ★

"They were consulting an oracle," he told Prescott later. His voice was still quivering with fury. "One man had twisted the head from a live chicken and then clawed open its belly with his fingers. The bird was still flapping and the man was spreading its intestines on the dirt to read the future. It was barbaric, *vile!* I lost my temper and assaulted the men bodily. I threw them outside. I had difficulty in restraining myself from burning the hut around their ears."

"Don't be too hard on them," Prescott advised. "These people are going through mental agonies which even we cannot comprehend. They're facing possible genocide, and they must ask themselves why. You have to expect some stark soul-searching, a few backward steps."

"This was not a mere backward step," O'Keefe complained bitterly. "It was a total reversion. Tonight I felt myself in the presence of an ancient evil. Those heathens had gone back to that black kingdom of darkness which existed before we brought them the Love of God, and the knowledge and message of Jesus."

"Darkest Africa was a white man's myth," Prescott said. "Before the

191

Europeans penetrated the continent most African societies had their own religious faith and beliefs. The ceremonies and taboos at ground level were no more derogatory to the central belief of a Supreme God than those of any other religion. If they built Him no churches it was because He was considered too great to be contained in any man-made building. His abode was beyond the sky."

"They were filled with primitive superstition," O'Keefe said forcefully. "There was nothing more. Before the arrival of the Church the whole of Africa cried out for salvation."

"I don't agree." They had not argued for a long time and Prescott was beginning to enjoy the conflict of debate. "I'll concede that the churches have done an excellent job in terms of education, and in the medical and social fields, but I'm not so sure that the average African was clamouring to be saved. The kingdom of darkness you mentioned was not confined to Africa, it has recurred throughout the world and throughout the ages in men's souls, whenever there has been a major tyranny or war."

O'Keefe was still angry. "Do you really believe that they were happier in their ignorance, sacrificing to a fetish without any knowledge of the True Light of God?"

"I wouldn't put it as strongly as that." Prescott smiled briefly. "But I do believe there was much sacred to the African spirit which was destroyed too hastily in the rush to put Christianity in its place."

"And what was that?" O'Keefe demanded.

"God," Prescott suggested simply. "The African idea of God. We didn't introduce One God to them because they had always believed in One God. We merely persuaded them to abandon their racial mythology and accept our own. They traded spirits for angels, old dances for new hymns. They did so in a period of crisis when the white races seemed superior to their own. Now they face another armageddon, with the white races departed and the pendulums of power gone mad. I'm not surprised that they're questioning the new mythology and groping back to the old. The tragedy will come if they lose sight of the central reality in their confusion."

"Christianity is *not* a mythology!"

"Then call it a faith, a European faith — one that is perhaps not sufficient for Africa now that Africa is becoming African again. The African faith was deep-rooted but Christianity tore them out, and perhaps the roots of Christianity are too shallow in the African soil. This could be the real tragedy for this continent."

"If they forsake Christianity they are Godless — they have nothing to grope back to!"

O'Keefe realized he was shouting. He had drawn himself up to his full height and his huge fists were clenched. He felt a strong desire to punch Prescott hard on the nose.

Prescott took notice of the fighting stance. He stared at the priest with an uncertain expression of faint surprise. Then O'Keefe spun abruptly on his heel and strode away into the night.

9

MAXWELL stared up at the hospital ceiling as the familiar thunder of jet engines swept overhead. He wondered if they intended to bomb Bumaru and tasted the hot dryness of fear in his parched throat. He was sweating and the ward was silent as the black patients lay frozen to listen to the danger from above. Then from the foot of his bed Maxwell heard a small whimper of terror.

The sound came from Aliya. The child had been crawling on the hospital floor and now she was trying to drag herself under the bed. On impulse Maxwell leaned out and lifted her up. He brought the child into the bed beside him.

"Hush, baby," he murmured softly. "They'll go away."

It was a rash promise, but after a

moment the noise faded and the planes had gone. Aliya lay trembling before she finally dared to raise her head and stare at Maxwell with big, dark brown eyes. The American felt a sharp stab of conscience. Aliya was the other side of the picture, the ground-level reality no combat pilot could afford to know. Emotion choked his throat and they both lay still.

It was the beginning of a relationship. Every time the planes came near Aliya would take refuge in Maxwell's bed, and when the time came for them to learn to walk they walked together. The nuns had tried to teach Aliya to use a pair of tiny crutches and failed, but when she watched Maxwell hopping in crutches she was encouraged to try again. They took their tumbles together, but slowly learned to master the sticks and retain their balance.

★ ★ ★

As hunger closed its heartless grip around Biafra the ordinary Ibos began to die like flies swept by great gusts of insecticide. Each day was a desperate struggle to live through to the next, and at Bumaru the only exception was the Tuesday of each week when the food truck reached them from the central distribution point at Owerri. Sometimes the food truck was late, and sometimes it did not come at all. Then all bellies went empty.

On the Tuesday after Maxwell and Aliya had begun to walk the food truck was on time. It lurched out of the bush road and on to the dust of the compound before the church shortly before noon. The ancient Mercedes ground to a halt with a squeal of brakes and a hiss of steam from the radiator as the waiting refugees flocked forward on all sides. A babble of voices rose in begging cries and immediate altercation as the scramble began.

O'Keefe and Prescott were also alert to the truck's arrival. They knew that if they did not get there first then they would have a possible riot on their hands and any hope of fair distribution and the food lasting its allotted seven days would be gone. They had to force a passage through the jostling throng of black bodies that were mostly skin and bone, with Daniel, Isaac and Alif close at their heels.

The two men with the Mercedes were already trying to calm the crowd. The driver was a young African in a white shirt and grey trousers. His companion was an African priest with spectacles, a white collar and a worn and crumpled grey suit. They were old friends and O'Keefe greeted them warmly.

The greetings were necessarily brief due to the pressures of the crowd. O'Keefe soon had to turn and raise his hands in urgent appeal for quiet and patience. As he did so Mary Kerrigan and Sister Bernadette eased their way to the front of the crowd. Both the nun and the nurse were held in great respect and their presence helped to restrain the hungry refugees, especially the women who were normally more voluble than the men. Those who were shouting in anguish and holding up their pitifully undernourished babies became quiet when Sister Bernadette added her pleas for calm in their own language.

When order was restored Prescott climbed on to the back of the truck with Alif. O'Keefe succeeded in clearing a narrow gangway to the brick storehouse at the end of the accommodation block and unlocked the door. Mary took up a position there to guard the door while the first of the sacks of powdered milk, each one stamped with the symbol of the Red Cross, were passed down. Daniel and Isaac took one between them. O'Keefe lifted the second in his arms. Prescott tilted the third over the back edge of the truck where the African priest and his driver were waiting to receive it, and then he paused and raised his head.

He stared at the dusty track that led back through the bush and forest to the main road. He could hear the sound of approaching vehicles. They were coming at speed and suddenly every face was turned in the same direction. A jeep leaped out of the bush, followed by two large army trucks. The refugees screamed hysterically and scattered.

The jeep roared to a violent stop in the centre of the compound, its wheels showering dust clouds and dirt over the cowering women and children who were too weak or too lame to move quickly away. The trucks pulled up behind it and armed soldiers began to disembark. Some of them wore scraps of uniform, a forage cap, a webbing belt or army boots, while others wore tattered oddments of civilian shirts and shorts, were bare-footed or bare-chested. Their weapons ranged from modern automatic rifles and machine guns to a scattering of spears and machete knives.

The initial panic at their abrupt

appearance subsided slowly into an uncertain apprehension. It was not a Federal attack. The troops were not the dreaded Yoruba or Hausa, but fellow-Ibos. The limp flag that was lashed to the windscreen upright of the jeep fluttered the rising sun emblem of Biafra.

Prescott straightened up slowly on the back of the food truck. His instinct sensed trouble and he glanced at Alif standing uncertainly beside him. He made a warning, downward gesture with his hand which the boy understood and obeyed. Alif got down from the truck and moved to one side. Prescott remained.

The officer in charge of the troop detachment stood upright from his jeep, a tight-lipped and familiar figure. His new tunic had two sleeves, but after the long months of bitter fighting he had endured in the bush it was as torn and battle-stained as the old one had been. He still carried his left hand tucked inside his tunic, like a black Napoleon, but the captain's pips on his shoulders had been replaced by the rank insignia of a major.

John Okwela walked slowly forward to confront O'Keefe, his right hand resting casually on his holstered revolver.

"Good morning, Father," he said curtly. He had intended to address O'Keefe simply as 'Priest,' which would have been a calculated insult, but something inside which he could not control had stopped him at the last moment. Already he was angry with himself for his weakness.

O'Keefe had lowered the powdered milk sack to the ground. He straightened up and wiped a film of white dust from his black robe. He smiled at the man he had once regarded as a son.

"Good morning, John."

"You will address me by my rank." Okwela barked because he felt that he had face to make up with his men.

"Good morning, Major." O'Keefe maintained the same tone, although his smile was strained. "We are pleased to see you, as always. But with so many soldiers and so many guns, I fear that this is not just a courtesy visit. What do you want from us?"

"This food truck." Okwela said briefly. "There is a war in progress, and my soldiers are hungry. I am here to commandere these supplies."

O'Keefe stared at him, first with stunned disbelief and then with slowly rising anger. He looked round at the waiting soldiers, some were grinning and some were solemn-faced. They were not exactly fat but at least they were lean and healthy.

"Your men may be hungry," O'Keefe pointed out. "But these people — " He indicated the cautiously returning circle of refugees. "Your people! They are literally starving. If you take this food away they will die."

Okwela refused to move his head. He did not want to see the hollow, dull-eyed faces of the refugees.

"I am sorry," he said briefly. To a certain extent he was both sorry and ashamed, but he had made up his mind and he was adamant. "My soldiers must stay strong if they are to fight and defend their country. If the army starves there will be nothing to save Biafra. The Hausas will come and butcher you all. They burn every village they capture and there is no reason for them to spare Bumaru. The army must eat first!"

"The military ensures you receive adequate supplies," O'Keefe protested. "We only get what is left after the army has taken the lion's share. You cannot steal our food!"

"Our supplies were lost in a Federal attack. So we must take what we can find. These men must go back to the battlefront. Many of them will die anyway." Okwela's voice lifted with sudden passion and finished on a note of contempt. "The people here do nothing. I can pity the women and children but there are men here who are cowards."

His gaze shifted and he recognized Daniel.

"You — " He stormed. It was easy to transform his savage emotions into fury. "Are you still tending your pretty flowers while Biafra bleeds and our villages are turned into rotting graveyards? You pray to Jesus while our soldiers are slaughtered by the enemy, and through your prayers you hope to survive. You are a fool! And you are of no more use to Biafra than the vultures which feast on our corpses."

"John, please!" Sister Bernadette tried to calm him down. "We are your friends and this was your home."

"Be quiet," Okwela snapped. "I do not wish to argue with you."

"Then argue with me," Mary snapped back at him in the same tone. She pushed past Daniel and the nun and her freckled face was flushed red with anger. "You of all people should be the last person to come here to steal our supplies — "

"I do not steal. I commandere — "

"Steal!" Mary shouted at him. "These people raised you and yet you come back like a common thief to steal food from the starving. Have you no sense of gratitude? We fought here to save your arm. We nursed you when you were sick. Have you forgotten all that?"

"The arm," Okwela said bitterly, "Is dead and useless. You did not save it. I have only one arm."

"Perhaps you are lucky to have your life."

"Enough of this. I did not come here to talk."

With his right hand he thrust her roughly to one side. He took a pace forward and O'Keefe barred his way. They glared at each other, and then the bolt of a machine gun clicked loudly in the big hands of the Ibo sergeant with the first truck load of soldiers. The sound was repeated several times, a series of clearly audible warnings.

O'Keefe clenched his fists but stood back.

Okwela looked up to Prescott on the back of the food truck.

"Throw down the rest of the sacks," he commanded. "My men will load them on to their trucks."

"No." Prescott's voice was ice-cold but controlled. His face was carefully blank of expression. "I can't stop you, but I'll be damned if I'll help you."

Okwela's face contorted into a black thundercloud. He recognized Prescott with some surprise, and unexpectedly hate twisted his thick-lipped mouth.

"The Englishman," he snarled. "You are truly a fool to remain in Biafra. Your government supports the Nigerian massacre of the Ibos. British bombs are destroying Ibo villages, and British armoured cars are winning the Federal battles. London could tell Lagos to stop this war tomorrow, but they prefer to see the extermination of the Ibos."

His right hand clawed at his holster

and pulled out his revolver. He pointed it up at Prescott.

"Throw down those sacks," he commanded again. "Or I shall kill you!"

★ ★ ★

In the hospital Maxwell could not help but be aware of the commotion. His first thought was that the troops were searching for him, and there was a measure of relief when he realized they were after the food. He twisted on to his shoulder and watched through the window behind him. Okwela's soldiers were watching the drama around the food truck and the refugees had closed ranks behind him. The thatched roof over the verandah kept the hospital windows in deep shade so there was only a minimal risk that Maxwell's white face could be noticed.

Just in case the soldiers became wandering and inquisitive Maxwell reached over to the small locker beside his bed. Inside was his shirt, his boots and his belt, although his ruined trousers had been thrown away. Behind his boots, pushed out of sight and memory by a nun's nervous hand, was the Colt 0.45 in its holster. Maxwell pulled it out and laid it on the pillow beside him.

When he saw Okwela pull his revolver on Prescott, Maxwell tensed with alarm. By now he was well acquainted with everyone at the mission, they had all stopped frequently at his bedside to make cheerful conversation. He had no particular cause to help Prescott, but neither could he watch the man shot down in cold blood.

He slipped the Colt out of the holster and raised it to cover Okwela.

A black hand with slim, delicate fingers rested lightly on his shoulder.

"Please, no," Sister Ruth begged him softly. "They will kill you too, and if they shoot into the hospital many of our patients will be hurt."

Maxwell turned his head. Her face

was filled with sadness and fear. Behind her Aliya was peering with frightened eyes from the uncertain safety of the nun's skirts.

Maxwell nodded slowly and lowered the gun.

Sister Ruth gripped her crucifix and began to pray.

* * *

Prescott stared into the murderous face of Okwela and suddenly he was afraid. He had never expected to be afraid to die. It came to all men, the end of an episode, the beginning of an even greater spiritual adventure. He hoped that his fear was for the agony of dying, and not for death itself.

He stood on the truck and waited. He knew that he would not throw down the food sacks, and he knew just as surely that Okwela would shoot him dead.

Okwela raised the revolver, tilting the barrel upward by another inch. His hand trembled, and Prescott imagined the black knuckle on the trigger turning white.

Then Mary Kerrigan screamed.

Okwela turned sharply, like a startled cat. He hadn't fired yet the scream had been a shriek of pure terror. Mary's face was white but she was not looking at him or at Prescott. The tight circle of refugees had hastily backed away again as it became apparent that Okwela intended to shoot, and his jeep, which had previously been hidden by the close-pressed bodies, was now clearly visible. Mary was staring at the bonnet of the jeep, where an African head wearing the peaked cap of a Federal army officer was mounted on a spike.

O'Keefe stepped forward, his face horrified. For a moment it was beyond belief, then he turned back to Okwela and demanded:

"John, what in God's name is this?"

"A battle trophy," Okwela said slowly. "The head of a Yoruba lieutenant. Colonel Ojukwu has decreed that every

Ibo must try to collect ten Nigerian heads."

"But this is the act of a savage. *You are a Christian.*"

"*Not any more!*" Okwela screamed back at him. "Not since the Hausas killed Victoria and my sons in Kano!"

O'Keefe's face softened with sudden compassion. "I guessed as much." His tone was gentle then filled with anguish. "John, you should have been able to tell us. We could have helped you in your grief. It should never have come to this."

"You would have helped me," Okwela said scornfully. "How, Father? By telling me to turn the other cheek? My wife, my sons, my arm! How many cheeks do I have to turn?"

"John, please — "

"Major." Okwela warned.

"Major, please listen to me."

"No, I have heard enough. You will shut up. You will all shut up!" He brandished his revolver in a circle and the refugees who had not already fled stampeded out of range.

"Major, this is the work of an animal but you are still a man. Even if you are no longer a Christian, even though you must fight — you do not have to become a beast."

"One more word and I will shoot *you!*" Okwela threatened.

He glared at O'Keefe for five ferocious seconds and then spun on his heel. "Sergeant," he shouted in Ibo. "Detail two men to drive the food truck back to our camp. We will take all of it and unload it ourselves. If anyone tries to intervene you will shoot them."

The big sergeant stepped forward and snapped at two of his men. The machine gun was slung on a strap over his shoulders and swung easily in his hands. The soldiers he singled out walked lazily to the mission truck, grinning at each other as they climbed into the cab.

Okwela stalked back to his jeep. He slid into his seat beside his driver and rested his revolver on his knee. His left hand was an aggravating dead weight inside his tunic. He was always more conscious of it during a crisis. For a few moments he sat and sulked, staring through the dirty windscreen at the severed head.

Prescott looked over a dozen heads at the sergeant with the machine gun. Sister Bernadette reached up and tugged gently at his hand.

"Come down, Geoffrey," she advised.

Prescott glanced back into the truck, at the stacked cartons of corned beef and egg powder, and the sacks of *garri* flour. He was bitter but he climbed down from the truck, contriving to tip off the sack of milk powder that was balanced on the tailboard before the truck drove away.

The jeep followed the Mercedes out of the compound and Okwela did not look back.

The sergeant stared doubtfully at Prescott and the one defiant sack which had split open in the dust. Then he shrugged and turned away. He and his men climbed back into their vehicles.

When the dust had cleared the compound was empty of soldiers. Only hunger and a terrible silence remained.

10

EVERY week they dug a score of graves at Bumaru, but during the week following Okwela's visit, before the next food truck came, the total reached fifty-nine.

The hospital now suffered a forty percent death rate and the beds were badly needed. As soon as possible Maxwell moved out to share the guest bungalow with Prescott, and as he became more mobile and confident on his crutches he helped out with any work he was capable of doing.

Sister Bernadette watched them one morning from the hospital verandah. Prescott and O'Keefe were lifting up a cross timber for a new lean-to shelter needed to protect the exposed refugees from the torrential rains. Maxwell and Alif were steadying the upright posts which had already been planted in the hard red earth. Maxwell worked with one hand, having abandoned his right crutch. He and Prescott were both stripped to the waist and browned by the sun. Their ribs were as easily counted as those of the Africans. When the cross timber was in place Daniel and Isaac jumped nimbly up on to the trestles and hammered it fast with six inch nails.

"Just look at them a moment," the nun said quietly to Mary who had stopped beside her. "A Catholic priest, an agnostic, and a mercenary; and yet here they are labouring together at the work of God. Isn't it something to think about?"

Mary nodded. She watched as Prescott and O'Keefe picked up another timber, but mostly her eyes were on Maxwell as he limped over to the next corner post.

"None of them are easy men to understand," she observed. "I thought I hated the American for what he was, but he's helped Aliya to walk which

218

is something we failed to do. Geoff can be insufferable with his opinions, but it's hardly accurate to call him an agnostic, and he's definitely a long way from being atheist. And Father O'Keefe — " She paused.

"Liam O'Keefe works like an Irish navvy, and sometimes he is terribly tempted to fight in the same way." Sister Bernadette laughed. "Those big fists were never intended for a priest."

Mary smiled with her. They watched for another minute before turning to the rows of human need that waited for them inside the hospital.

★ ★ ★

By nightfall the new shelter was half complete. Maxwell, Prescott and O'Keefe returned to it the next morning to finish thatching the roof. The three African boys were nowhere to be seen but they had left a large pile of long grasses cut the day before and so the three men began without them.

Maxwell passed the bundles of grass up to Prescott and O'Keefe and an hour passed before the supply was exhausted. O'Keefe swung down to earth with a puzzled frown on his face.

"The boys must have overslept," he said doubtfully. "I'll see if I can find them."

"Okay." Maxwell was grateful for the rest. He lowered himself to a sitting position with his back to a post and Prescott squatted down beside him.

O'Keefe left them in idle conversation. He began his search with the dining room, hoping to find the mission boys at breakfast. They were not there so he tried the dormitory room they shared further along the accommodation block. Again it was empty. He spotted one of the smaller mission boys but before he could call out a question the boy made a guilty start and ducked out of sight. O'Keefe was suddenly worried. He began to search more urgently around the remaining buildings and

220

among the swarm of refugees in the compound.

Finally it was Sister Alice who brought Rachel to see him. The nun kept a comforting arm around the younger girl's shoulders. Rachel had been crying and her face was still tear-stained. O'Keefe knew that she was very close to Daniel, they were still children but he had hopes that one day he would be called upon to perform the marriage ceremony for them. Now one glance was sufficient to tell him that catastrophe had occurred. Rachel's world had fallen apart.

O'Keefe hurried to meet them and took the girl's hands in his own.

"Tell me," he said as gently as possible.

"Daniel has gone to fight." Rachel broke into another flood of tears. "Ever since John Okwela called him a coward he has been convinced that he must leave here and join the army. I have argued with him but last night he made up his mind. I would have told you, but I could not really believe it. This morning he has gone. He did not even say goodbye!"

"Alif and Isaac have gone with him," Sister Alice finished for her. "I have looked everywhere but they are nowhere to be found."

"Oh, God," O'Keefe said slowly. "My children." His hand touched Rachel's black curls. "My poor child."

For a moment he closed his eyes, and then he raised eyes, hands and voice to the blinding blue sky and shouted in anguished rage.

"They are only boys! *Suffer the little children to come unto me!* Why? Why? Why?"

The echoes flew around the compound in mockery. The huddled groups of refugees stared back at him but made no answer. Slowly O'Keefe lowered his hands and his shoulders slumped in despair.

★ ★ ★

David Katsina stood upright in his Saladin armoured car, careless of possible snipers as he held field glasses to his eyes and stared down the corpse-littered road to where the ruins of the next Ibo village were smouldering beneath a pall of thick smoke. His fearless pose was strongly characteristic. He would survive as a hero with nerves of steel, or not at all. He had made that decision at the beginning. Behind him were three more Saladins in close support, and then three Saracen armoured personnel carriers each carrying ten of his fully armed troops. The boats and canoes of the first sea-borne invasion were far behind and now his commando was motorized again.

It had been a long, gruelling slog up from Port Harcourt. The stubborn Biafrans had resisted every step of the way, mass grave pits accommodated their corpses along every mile of the road, and their guerrilla fighters played havoc behind the advancing Federal lines. After a year of beastial civil war Katsina, now Major Katsina, had acquired a grudging respect for the enemy. He had no pity, but he had to admit they died hard.

Over the past months the tactics of the war had changed. With newly imported Russian Ilyushin jets flattening the Biafran towns and villages with bombs from on high there was no need for the heavy pounding of artillery shells to precede each attack. Instead the Federal army advanced behind the faster shock waves of armoured cars. The Biafrans vacated the villages, the women and children fleeing deeper into the shrinking Biafran territory while their men fought back from the forest and bush.

Katsina had earned his promotion to major. He personally led his commando into every battle, setting a tough example which every man was expected to follow. He was merciless and his discipline was harsh. Slackers in his ranks were pistol-whipped or flogged.

Cowards and deserters were shot. Prisoners were never taken. His men called him Tiger Katsina because of his eyes, and to his great satisfaction the name had been picked up by the Nigerian and European press. Whenever he was obliged to talk to a war reporter Katsina would laugh and proudly boast that he was the only Tiger in Africa.

He was confident now of an eventual Federal victory. Politics and economics were not his strongest subjects but he was shrewdly aware that British oil interests would ensure the massive continued flow of arms and ammunition Nigeria needed to finish this war. His only concern was that it should not finish too quickly. A few more months and he was certain to be at least a lieutenant colonel.

After a concentrated study he was satisfied with what he saw. The barrage of shells from the 76 mm guns of the three Saladins had finished the work begun by the Russian bombers and there was no sign of any remaining resistance. A few injured men were still crawling for cover and the village was in flames. He lowered the field glasses and glanced back over his shoulder. His teeth gleamed white as he made a flamboyant forward movement with his arm. Then he slid down through the turret into the driving seat.

Seconds later K Company was moving at speed down the narrow road. With Katsina's Saladin in the lead the armoured force burst into the shattered village with all machine guns blazing. One Ibo martyr ran forward from the roadside with a flame-spluttering beer bottle in his hand, but before the crude petrol bomb could be thrown he was eviscerated by bullets. A crawling Ibo with broken legs tried to drag himself faster but then he was hammered into the mud only inches from the safety of the bush. A pregnant woman ran screaming from a collapsed hut and her fat belly exploded like a blood and gut inflated balloon.

As the armoured cars hit the village they fanned out and roared to a stop. Katsina's vehicle faced forward, the others had veered to right and left. Immediately the turrets swivelled as the gunners raked the surrounding tree-tops for the inevitable snipers. On the return swing they raked the bush and forest at ground level. The village had been abandoned but the bush was thick with the enemy.

The Saracens had halted just before the village and rapidly disembarked the ground troops who dashed into the jungle on either side of the road. Then the heavier personnel carriers sped on to add their machine gun firepower to the spearhead of Saladins. The commandos mopped up with a calculated pincer action on both flanks.

The battle was short and furious, a routine pattern before the Biafrans melted back into the forest. Then abruptly the unexpected happened. A Biafran jeep bolted from cover between two of the burning thatched huts and made a desperate race for the exit road leading out of the far side of the village.

It was a forlorn hope. Katsina was by then operating the second machine gun fixed to the commander's cupola and his sharp eyes spotted the jeep the instant it emerged to make its break for freedom. He swung the muzzle round and fired joyfully. Bullets crashed into the jeep and it swerved violently as the driver died at the wheel. The vehicle ploughed through the remains of a mud wall and then exploded into a roaring furnace of red and yellow flames.

The firing from the forest had stopped. The engagement was over and after a pause Katsina drew his revolver and climbed out of the turret. He dropped to the earth and strolled casually to examine the blazing jeep. The air was blistering hot, filled with drifting smoke and cordite. There was silence except for the fierce crackle of the flames, and the terrible, agonized screaming from inside the jeep.

The driver was definitely dead, a Biafran officer recognizable by the peaked cap which had fallen forward over his face. The screams came from a woman passenger who was still alive.

There was a movement beside him. Katsina half turned and saw Lieutenant Agama, his new junior officer who had led the ground troops. Agama was another Yoruba and another ex-Sandhurst cadet. He was brave and he showed promise, but he had only been in the front line for a few weeks. His grave young face was uncertain beneath the green rim of his helmet.

"Shouldn't we pull her out?" He asked in English.

Katsina looked back for the pressmen who frequently accompanied the tail end of the back-up forces now arriving. There was no white face in sight, no sign of a camera, and no one who looked even remotely like a foreign journalist.

"We might get burned," Katsina said. His cheerful tone made it a joke.

Agama hesitated. The screaming was a hideous, brain-drilling sound as the trapped woman was roasted alive. He stepped forward with his revolver but Katsina checked his arm.

"Why waste a bullet?" The major smiled and again used his impeccable Sandhurst voice. "She is only an Ibo whore!"

The hardened commandos who had gathered to watch laughed their approval. They did not understand the words but they loved the hilarious plum-in-mouth accent.

In this war the quality of mercy did not exist.

★ ★ ★

The embattled heartland of Biafra was by now totally dependent upon the vast international relief effort that had been launched by the International Red Cross, the World Council Of Churches, the Save The Children Fund and Oxfam. The normal crops of yams, cassava and other staple foods were eaten or destroyed and no new crops were planted. Only world charity kept the Ibos alive, but inevitably the relief work was bedevilled by corruption, mismanagement, bungling, and above all by the sheer bloody-minded obstinacy of the military politicians.

In Lagos General Gowon's Federal Government insisted that the only mercy food supplies allowed into Biafra must travel in lorry convoys over authorized land routes which Federal troops could supervise. Air flights which began outside Federal control could carry more arms than food and would be shot down by Federal artillery.

In Aba, the capital of Biafra since the fall of Enugu, Colonel Ojukwu's Rebel Republic replied that they would not permit hostile troops free access to their besieged country and neither would they accept food supplies which could be poisoned en route. Only airlifted supplies were acceptable.

While the General and the Colonel

engaged in hot propoganda speeches for the benefit of the outside world the skeleton babies of Biafra died in their thousands.

At Bumaru the trickle of supplies dwindled, and was finally cut off. The army did not raid them again, but another Tuesday came when the relief truck from Owerri did not arrive. They waited for a full week until the last handfuls of *garri* flour were gone. Then there was nothing. The next Tuesday came but still there was no sign of the relief lorry. Wednesday came and Thursday came. There was nothing to distribute and they dug more rows of graves.

In the village the Africans ate cassava leaves and hunted the last of the lizards and the rats.

In the compound there was a listless silence, a waiting for death. Only the spectre of famine walked.

"This is murder," O'Keefe said in torment. His black robe hung in surplus folds on his own wasted frame and his eyes were deep hollows of grief as he looked over his huddled flocks. "The radio tells us that there is food rotting on the docksides at Lagos. Thousands of tons of food are stockpiled in the warehouses on Fernanda Po, and yet these people must starve while the politicians wrangle over how it can be delivered. This is worse than what Hitler did to the Jews!"

"It must end soon." Prescott tried to give him hope. "Aba is encircled and under shellfire. When it falls Owerri and Umuahia will be the only towns left. The war must end."

"For so many of these people it will be too late." O'Keefe pointed to a woman squatting in the dust. She was too weak to move with her mouth too parched to even moan. A shrivelled boy child lay across her knee with grey hair and skin which had turned a grotesque white through malnutrition. "Those two will die tomorrow, and a dozen more."

"There's an airstrip at Uli," Maxwell

said slowly. "They've rigged up some kind of makeshift runway that's still operational. According to last night's radio there are still a few planes getting through to make night landings."

★ ★ ★

Prescott and O'Keefe took the Land Rover to make the twenty mile drive. Their last quest for food had left them sick at heart but it was nothing to the war-ravaged horrors of human degradation they witnessed on the road to Uli. The refugees who choked the roads were no longer a live nation fleeing in panic from advancing terror, they were crawling corpses, ghosts in grey rags, zombies from the graveyards of dead hope where the terrors had already overtaken them. Before O'Keefe had wept, but now he was dry of tears. Fatigue and familiarity had dulled his eyes and his senses. Even the soul of a priest could only take its fill of pain, and then the pain overflowed and there was room for no more.

The airstrip at Uli proved to be a converted road where the jungle had been cleared back on either side to a maximum width of some seventy-five feet. Rows of oil drums marked the flare path. The Land Rover was halted at a roadblock and a young Biafran lieutenant escorted them to a hut on the edge of the jungle. Here they found a Biafran major in command and two African relief workers. The only white man present was another priest, a small, wiry, blue-eyed man with deeply grooved temples and wisps of grey hair.

"Father Flanaghan," O'Keefe said warmly, and the two priests shook hands. They were old friends, but Flanaghan was weary and his grip was hesitant, and suddenly O'Keefe was ashamed of his need to beg. "We've come for food," he blurted awkwardly. "We're all starving at Bumaru."

"The whole of Biafra is starving." Flanaghan answered.

"Yes, Timothy, but at Bumaru there is nothing, absolutely nothing! We haven't a single handful of *garri* left."

"Your distribution centre is Owerri," Flanaghan said patiently. "We keep records of all the centres and how many camps each centre has to serve. We try to keep an approximate record of how many new refugees have flowed into each camp so the food that is available can be distributed fairly."

"Bumaru is dying," O'Keefe said simply. "The people are trying to eat leaves and choking. All we do now is dig graves."

"Liam, I know. Every camp has to bury its quota of dead every day. There just isn't enough food to go round."

"Timothy, it isn't a question of quotas. By the end of the week you can send in a bulldozer and bury us all!"

"Liam, have pity on me!" Flanaghan cried in anguish. "Don't you realize that here I am not just a servant of God, *I am God!* The little food that passes through my hands is life or death, and I have to decide who lives and who dies. You ask me to give you food here and now, but if I do I must take it from supplies destined elsewhere and condemn others to death. You should not ask me to make such a choice. Go back to Bumaru and wait for your share to come through Owerri!"

O'Keefe faltered, but Prescott had no pity. He had come for food and he did not intend to return empty-handed.

"Our share has not been coming through Owerri," he said grimly. "If you've sent anything intended for Bumaru then it must have been diverted. We haven't had anything from Owerri for two weeks."

"If the food has gone astray after leaving here then it's not my responsibility. You should have gone to Owerri."

"But we didn't," Prescott snapped. He threw in a lie and didn't care a damn. "We came here and we haven't got enough petrol to go back to Owerri.

You've got to give us something here."

"If I do that then everyone will come here. There has to be some system of distribution to be fair."

"The system has broken down. You can't deny us!"

Prescott was shouting and O'Keefe seized his arm.

"Geoffrey, please!"

"*Bumaru is starving.* If we go back with nothing we all perish."

Flanaghan bowed his head. "Famine is everywhere. Biafra is a country forsaken by God."

"You are God," Prescott reminded him. "You have the power to give or deny, and we are here with a Land Rover to receive."

There was silence. When Flanaghan raised his head the temple lines were deeper, his complexion was grey with grief and the blue eyes were beaten.

"Our position is desperate, Timothy." O'Keefe spoke with compassion. "We would not press you if there were any other choice."

Flanaghan nodded slowly. "Alright, Liam, I'll give you what I can. There's a Constellation due to land later tonight."

"God bless you."

"May He bless us all."

★ ★ ★

The night proved dark, with heavy cloud and a steamy mist lingering at ground level after the evening rain. Prescott and O'Keefe stood outside the wooden hut with Flanaghan and the two African relief workers and waited. All of them were staring upward with tense, anxious faces. The Constellation was due an hour after midnight but the pilot would have to run the gauntlet of Federal artillery and Mig fighters and so the flights were never on time.

"Sometimes," Flanaghan admitted sadly, "They do not come at all."

They could not see another soul but they were not alone. The damp darkness breathed the invisible presence

239

of men all around the perimeter of the jungle airstrip. Most of them were Biafran soldiers, the others were more missionaries and medical teams who had arrived with the last hours of daylight.

In the adjoining section of the hut which served as a radio room they could hear the low mutter of voices, the Biafran major and his radio operator crouched over the big transmitter and waiting for the vital radio code signal from the thick blanket of darkness overhead. They were the only sound except for the inevitable nocturnal squeaks and rustlings from the surrounding forest.

"The plane will come from Sao Tome," Flanaghan said in a whisper, as though afraid to break the silence. "It will have to cross the Gulf of Guinea and then make a wide circle over Cameroon to come in from the east. It is the safest route."

They stared east. The back of Prescott's neck began to ache and when he moved his head he found the muscles were stiff. O'Keefe stood calmly with his feet spaced and his hands clasped around his crucifix. Flanaghan constantly shifted his feet and slapped at an insect which had singled him out for special attention. The two Africans were the shadows of carved images in the gloom, only their white shirts marked their position. Prescott began to massage the back of his neck with his hand.

The voices in the radio room had fallen silent, but after an hour of waiting they became audible again, sharper and more excited than before. A new, thin metallic voice was mixed in with the crackle of radio static.

Prescott lifted his head and stared again into the thick darkness. Two minutes passed and then he heard the drone of engines. The aircraft was there, flying without lights somewhere above the clouds. O'Keefe and Flanaghan prayed, and Prescott hoped that God was listening.

Ibo voices chattered suddenly in the night. Orders were shouted and hidden figures hurried to their set tasks. The landing lights flared in two bright rows on either side of the runway and a guiding beacon suddenly stabbed at the sky, the probing beam failed to penetrate the banks of grey cloud.

The plane was roaring low, a thunder of engines that seemed to be immediately over their heads. Prescott ducked and covered his ears. Abruptly the Constellation switched on its powerful landing lights. Already it was down to treetop level and the pilot had a split second to decide whether he could make it now or whether he had to climb for a second try. Every second of delay increased the danger of a Mig attack and the blaze of lights plunged down as the throttles were cut back.

For a few seconds there was nothing but the brilliant dazzle of the lights, the deafening crescendo of engine power and the scream of locked wheels. Prescott was blind in a great rush of displaced air and it seemed as though the Connie's wingtip slashed past within bare inches of his face. Then the sound rolled to a stop and the lights were extinguished as swiftly as they had appeared. The four, spinning turbo-props whirled to a standstill. For a moment the aircraft was silhouetted by the smokey light from the runway flares, and then they too spluttered and were put out. From the darkness on all sides desperate men converged.

Prescott led the rush, but came to an abrupt halt as a figure menaced him from the gloom. The young Biafran lieutenant barred the way with his revolver drawn and spoke curtly in English.

"Stay back! Priests must wait their turn."

O'Keefe's hand gripped Prescott's arm and they waited. An army truck snarled up out of the night and backed up to the open cabin door of the plane. Soldiers swung inside and after a few moments the first of a long series of heavy steel boxes was passed out. Prescott recognized the unmistakable shape of an ammunition box.

"It is always like this," Flanaghan said with the voice of resignation. "The arms take priority over the food."

The lieutenant heard and said sourly, "How do you think we are fighting this war — like savages with spears?"

When the truck had absorbed its load another took its place. Prescott watched with a sinking heart, feeling the sick weight of despair which cloaked the priests and relief workers around him. Every ammunition box meant less space for food, and the chain of steel boxes seemed endless. He calculated at least nine tons of arms, shells and bullets before the third truck pulled away and the soldiers climbed down from the aircraft. The lieutenant climbed up briefly to make a personal examination to satisfy himself that nothing of importance had been missed. Then he reappeared in the cabin doorway and waved the missionaries forward.

Prescott hauled himself up and then turned to help Flanaghan. They surveyed the stripped-down interior of the long cabin which was smothered in oil and littered with the rope lashings that had secured the arms cargo. At the far end of the cabin, occupying very little space, was a pile of sacks and cartons. They went closer.

"More bloody powdered milk," Prescott said in exasperation. "Don't they realize that half these bush Africans have no idea of how to mix it with water. They try to swallow it dry and then choke to death. We can't supervise them all."

"We must be grateful for what we can get," Flanaghan answered. "Here we are all beggars."

Prescott accepted the bitter truth and they began to unload. It was a job that was over all too quickly.

When he dropped to the runway again O'Keefe was waiting for him.

The food supplies had been carried over to the hut where they would be shared out after the plane had departed. O'Keefe drew Prescott to one side as Flanaghan hurried to supervise.

"Geoffrey — " O'Keefe was hesitant but he felt an obligation. "The aeroplane will be flying back empty. There's plenty of room if you still want to get out of Biafra. There's no need for you to stay."

Prescott looked up slowly at the dim outline of the propellers spiking the gloom above his head, and then at the nose cone of the aircraft where the pilot and co-pilot waited patiently at the controls behind darkened windows. The idea had occurred to him.

"We had trouble getting here," he said at last. "Alone you'd never get the Land Rover back to Bumaru."

"But you wanted to leave. It was only my sickness which prevented you leaving from Port Harcourt!"

Prescott smiled very faintly. "That was a long time ago, Father. Now it

246

doesn't seem so important." He put an arm around O'Keefe's shoulders and pulled him away from the runway. "Let's get back to the hut — we're delaying take-off."

11

DAWN flew in red banners over the Brigade HQ, each banner bright as a streak of blood, omens of the slaughter past and the slaughter still to come. On the dusty parade ground the three thin lines of Ibo boys stood to attention in ragged shorts and bare feet, listening intently to a brave and splendid speech by their officer. The youngest boy was twelve, the oldest was seventeen.

Daniel stood in the centre of the front line, proud and stiff with his chin held high. His shirt was wide open to show the amulet with his crocodile tooth fetish and the page from the New Testament which hung round his neck, and he was one of the few who had been entrusted with an old bolt action Lee Enfield rifle. On either side of him stood Isaac and Alif. They were the tallest three in the ranks and height gave them seniority. Isaac had another ancient rifle. Alif had only his bare hands. For all the boys their only insignia was a twist of grass tied around the left forearm to show that they were soldiers. The bold shoulder flashes with the Biafran sun, like so many of the men who had worn them, were a dim, almost forgotten memory.

Major John Okwela was the Biafran officer. He stood with his back to the rising sun, his face shadowed by the peak of his cap. His feet were exactly twelve inches apart. His left hand was tucked inside his tunic, while his right held a swagger stick which he thwacked gently against his right leg.

He gazed along the lines of alert young faces and his heart was heavy. These were the reinforcements who were to replace the battle losses in the previous days of fierce and bitter fighting. This was all he had to replace the glorious combat-hardened Twelfth Division which had been virtually annihilated after Aba had fallen and the Federal onslaught had rolled on in great waves of iron and steel toward Owerri.

He did not recognize Daniel who was straining to be noticed. He had a duty to perform and so he squared his shoulders and put on a confident smile. Daniel beamed at him in return.

"Soldiers of Biafra!" Okwela cried. "Can you stop the advance of the enemy and throw him back from our country?"

"*Yes, sir!*" shouted the boys in one voice. They had been primed by previous speeches and knew what was required.

"Can you avenge all our people who died in the massacres in the north?"

"*Yes, sir!*"

"Can you avenge all your fathers and brothers who have died in this war?"

"*Yes, sir!*"

"Can you avenge all the villages that have been burned? And all the old men, and women, and children who have been butchered by the Federal soldiers?"

"*Yes, sir! Yes, sir!*" The young throats screamed.

Okwela paused. There was sweat on his face, he could feel it but he hoped they could not see it. His voice wanted to choke but he smiled more broadly and pushed on:

"Soldiers of Biafra, what will you do when you see a Hausa man?"

"*Kill him!*" The trained response was immediate.

"What will you do when you see a Yoruba man?"

"*Kill him!*"

"What will you do when you see an armoured car?"

"*Destroy it!*"

Okwela stopped again and stared at the blurred lines of their faces. He was a murderer. If he borrowed the machine gun from his big sergeant who stood a yard to one side and cut them all to bloody pieces here and now he would be no less their executioner. He thwacked his own leg more ferociously with his stick and forced back the edges of his smile.

"Soldiers of Biafra, you know what you must do. Those of you who have guns will kill the enemy. The others will pick up the weapons from the dead Federal soldiers and we shall all go on to kill more of the enemy. Can we return victorious?"

"*Yes, sir! Yes, sir! Yes, sir!*" It was a primitive chant and their bare feet began to stamp in rhythm.

"Then go to your trucks." Okwela pointed his stick to the far side of the parade ground where the vehicles waited to take them up to the battlefront. "Go quickly, and kill all the Hausa and Yoruba!"

The boys ran with enthusiasm to board the trucks.

Daniel carried his rifle in one hand and in the other three bullets. Isaac had two bullets. Most of the other boys with rifles had one bullet each. Biafra was in its death throes and bullets were used up even faster than food. Bullets were scarce.

Okwela watched as the trucks drove away. His jeep was waiting but it was a faster vehicle and there would be time to catch up. He turned away and went to his quarters, slamming the door shut. There he sat down behind his desk and rested his face in his hands.

Alone he began to weep. His tears were long and bitter.

★ ★ ★

On the road back to Bumaru the Land Rover had bogged down for the third time. It was Prescott's turn to push and he got out to let O'Keefe take over the wheel. The sun was hot and savage on his shoulders and the nearside back wheel of the Land Rover was down to the hub in a mud-filled pot hole. Prescott scowled at it and then wielded a machete on the close-packed bush at the roadside. He stuffed the cut branches into the mud hole. Finally he threw the machete blade first into the earth and put his shoulder to the back of the Land Rover.

"Try it now," he shouted to O'Keefe. The priest looked back and nodded. He engaged low gear and four-wheel drive and eased gently off the clutch pedal. The Land Rover moved forward and the wheel began to spin. During the night twelve more aircraft had succeeded in making the dangerous night landing at Uli, and from the trickles of food that had come in with the continuous flow of arms Father Flanaghan had been able to spare them enough sacks and cartons to fill the Land Rover. The vehicle was heavily laden and Prescott had to lift and push with all his strength.

"Hard down!" he bawled.

O'Keefe pushed his foot hard down. The Land Rover lurched and the cut branches were sucked under the wheel. Prescott heaved and the wheel gripped. The Land Rover charged free. Prescott staggered and his hat fell into the mud. He swore as he massaged his aching back.

After a minute he collected the machete and his mud-stained hat and walked up to the Land Rover. He collapsed into the passenger seat beside O'Keefe and closed his eyes.

"Any worse than that and we'll have to start unloading her," he said wearily.

O'Keefe nodded and they sat in silence. They both needed the rest. Five minutes passed before O'Keefe straightened up and reached for the ignition. He hesitated and glanced at his slow-breathing companion. There were still mysteries about Prescott. After all this time some parts of the man were still an enigma.

O'Keefe said slowly. "Were you ever married, Geoffrey?"

"Once," Prescott said. "But Kenya during Mau Mau was a hard time for army wives. They were alone too often for too long, and all they had to do was wait and be scared. Sometimes the men they waited for were only wrecks or shadows of the men who went away. My wife couldn't take it. She went back to England. Eventually there was another man, inevitably a divorce."

His lips twitched a smile although he didn't open his eyes. "She married the other man, a nice, safe senior accountant with a respectable job in the City of London. They had a comfortable home in the stockbroker belt in Surrey. Ironically he died of a heart attack at forty-seven, while I survived the Mau Mau with a whole skin, and, I hope, a sane mind." He paused, then continued. "I was sorry for her, but it was too late to pick up the old pieces. Our marriage had lasted twelve years, and her betrayal when I needed her most had hit hard. She was weak, but I didn't know how to forgive her."

"Were there any children?"

"No, we tried in the early years but

she couldn't conceive."

Prescott opened his eyes and looked at O'Keefe.

"These are questions I didn't expect from you. Once I thought — perhaps even hoped — that Mary Kerrigan would ask them. Instead she asked Hank. He was married too, but his wife died. Our American friend has become quite fond of Mary, and I think it's mutual."

O'Keefe refused to be side-tracked. He said carefully, "I suppose I'm trying to understand you, Geoffrey. What I really wanted to ask is why are you still here? When you could be safe in Sao Tome, or even Lisbon by now."

Prescott sat up and stared forward. He was deep in thought but there were no tangible answers. O'Keefe waited patiently.

"I feel needed at Bumaru," Prescott said at last. "Perhaps it's as simple as that. The book I was writing, all that fascination with the past, Benin, the slave trade, the old Africa, it all seems unimportant now." He stopped to search his mind again, and then struggled on: "Perhaps I also feel that I owe something to Africa and the Africans. I fought in one African war, and there's a lot of African blood on my hands."

He turned his head to look directly at O'Keefe.

"Perhaps we all owe them something, Father, in return for all the things that our race has taken away from theirs. Do you remember the old African belief — *'The white man told us to close our eyes and pray, and when we opened them again we found that he had stolen our country!'*"

"I remember," O'Keefe said. "But there were two white men, the priest and the trader."

"They both robbed the African. The trader stole the wealth of the physical land beneath his feet. The priest tried to strip all the old poetry and myth from his mind and throw them all away. I concede that it was done with love and the best of intentions, but it was a rejection of all things African which may have caused the greatest harm. Now the white man has withdrawn and we have this terrible power struggle in the vacuum he left behind, and perhaps somewhere in the midst of all this the black man is also struggling to rediscover his soul — trying to balance what has been given with what was taken away."

O'Keefe was silent, for once he was not prompted to contest Prescott's view.

A minute passed and Prescott went on: "All around us there's a bloodbath, but there's always blood at a birth and modern Africa is in the process of being re-born. Africa had a past with empires and civilizations long before the white man came, and I believe it has a mighty future now that he has departed. There'll be more wars and bloodshed on this troubled continent, but Africa has great potential when she finds her new values and develops all her resources of raw material. We shall not live to see it, but there will be new civilizations in Africa, richer than any that have been before."

"And where is God — " O'Keefe asked gently, " — In this new vision of Africa?"

"He'll be there." Prescott smiled with conviction. "Perhaps under another name, or cloaked in a new philosophy. God does not belong to any one religion, Father. His children are all who are moral, just and compassionate, and who have faith — regardless of the name they call Him, the doctrine they attribute to Him, or the mythology they weave around Him."

"I thought you didn't believe in God, but in evolution?"

Prescott smiled again. "A baby evolves, from a spoonful of seed into a man like you and I, but somewhere it must have a father. Consequently I've never quite seen the logic of the eternal battle between the disciples of God and the disciples of evolution. Evolution can only tumble the taboos, the doctrines, the mythology of religions, it does not necessarily deny the core of God Himself. You believe God created the heavens and the earth. I believe He guided their evolution. Is there really such a gulf between us?"

"I don't know." O'Keefe was tired and he smiled wryly. "Perhaps you're doing to me what we did to the Africans. Have you thought about that?" He switched on the ignition and finished. "But we're still fifteen miles from Bumaru, and the people there are hungry."

* * *

The boys saw the black smoke puffs and heard the first shellbursts as they passed Owerri. In the hot blue sky overhead there were more Migs than vultures, flashing steel darts more graceful and more deadly than any carrion eater or prey bird, all of them swooping, diving, bombing and machine-gunning. They were systematically turning Biafra into a massacre of the guilty and the innocents.

Daniel's mouth was dry as he stared upward. He took a tighter grip on his rifle and with his free hand he fingered the fetish around his neck. Beside him Isaac and Alif were trembling.

The road was packed solid with refugees and wounded soldiers. Men and women struggled with crying children, baskets, bedsteads and suit-cases. Abandoned babies howled in the jostling human throng. The shell-shocked were screaming in frenzy, others dragged themselves in silence. There were soldiers in bloodied bandages, soldiers with crutches, soldiers with missing limbs, and incredibly one soldier holding a saline drip above his own arm as he staggered along.

Okwela's jeep had overtaken the trucks and now its horn was blaring constantly as it tried to clear a path through the mob. Progress was slow until they were past Owerri, and then suddenly there were only the demoralized soldiers, the fleeing remnants of a crushed army.

They were racing through plantations of oil palms and they were within range of the Federal artillery. A howitzer shell screamed over the bright green tops of the palms and exploded by the roadside. The palm trunks toppled and earth, palm fronds and flame spurted from the crater. The boys cowered down in the back of their open trucks, terror-stricken as the trucks raced on.

More shells exploded on both sides and suddenly the trucks skidded to a violent stop. Okwela's jeep had lurched off the road to avoid the burning wreckage of a field ambulance and the road was blocked.

Okwela ran back and shouted to the boys to get down from the trucks.

"Spread out and go forward," he ordered. "The battlefield is down this road. When you see the Hausa man, kill him! When you see the Yoruba man, kill him! You are the heroes who must save Biafra now!"

The boys faltered. Their cheer-leaders made no response. Many of them simply stared at the burned corpses spilled around the still smouldering ambulance.

Daniel felt sick, but he had been given a rifle and three bullets and he was the leader of the group. Okwela had still not recognized him, but the taunts over the flower beds still rankled. He lifted his rifle and shouted the words of the battle song they had been singing when they left the parade ground. He ran forward and Isaac and Alif ran loyally beside him. The other boys followed more slowly, fanning out through the palm trees as Okwela had commanded.

Okwela ran back to his jeep and scrambled inside. He drew his revolver and snapped at his driver to find a route through the plantation and keep pace with the boys. The wheels chewed up dirt as the jeep reversed with a clutch-slipping roar, and then it headed down the nearest track.

★ ★ ★

The cordite-choked, oil-smelling interior of the armoured car was hotter than an oven in hell, but David Katsina was supremely happy as he drove down the pitted road between the palms. The Biafran front line had snapped under the merciless Federal blitzkrieg that had followed the fall of Aba, and Katsina had been one of the first to exploit the gap. His superbly-armed, blood-lusting K Company commando had steam-rolled over the shattered Biafran defences. Now they were great steel cats among the panic-stricken Ibo mice, and soon Biafra would cease to exist.

The armoured cars were advancing on a wide front, but not in a direct line. Instead they were chasing back and forth and zig-zagging right and left with all guns blazing as they flushed out the last pockets of resistance. Most of the Biafran soldiers had not eaten for three days and without ammunition their morale had at last collapsed. There were crack battalions of Hausa infantry coming up behind but the armoured cars intended to hog all the glory.

A splutter of bullets came from the palm trees to his left and Katsina spun the Saladin towards them. A few of the bullets pinged and ricocheted off the steel flanks and then Katsina's gunner returned the fire with a long, raking burst. Two Ibo soldiers rolled dead from cover and a third broke out in a weaving run through the palm trunks. The running man was trying to escape with a bren gun but the weapon weighed him down. Another burst from the Saladin ripped him open and smashed him to the earth.

Katsina grinned his tiger grin and his tiger eyes were bright and fierce with elation. His gunner whooped in triumph.

* * *

Daniel ran for a hundred yards, veering left and right away from the terrifying shell explosions on either side. Then he heard the shrieking howl of a diving aircraft and looked up through the green fronds of the palm trees. He saw a Mig fighter coming down with rockets and cannon blazing and threw himself flat. The Mig swept overhead and a clump of amputated palm fronds crashed down on to Daniel's shoulders. Earth spurted all around and the pulpy sap oozed from the slashed trees.

When the plane had gone Daniel struggled up. Half the boys had already deserted and six more turned and fled. Daniel could feel his heart pounding and his limbs were like jelly but he stumbled forward and led the remainder on.

They burst out on to a dirt track

and saw the first armoured car. It was racing at full speed towards them and they turned to scurry back into the trees. Machine gun bullets cut down the stragglers and one thirteen-year-old was left screaming and writhing in agony.

Daniel stumbled into cover behind a palm trunk, turned, and crouched with the Lee Enfield at his shoulder. He saw the armoured car hurtle past and pulled the trigger. The kick of the gun slammed the butt back at his shoulder and knocked him flying. He felt as though his shoulder was broken and lay groaning in agony.

Alif appeared beside him and reached for the fallen rifle. Daniel swore and bit back his tears as he clawed the Lee Enfield from Alif's hands.

"You get a weapon from a dead Hausa man," he cried hysterically. "You don't steal mine!"

"I am sorry."

Alif was both embarrassed and ashamed. He helped his friend to stand and they both stared all around. They were alone in the palm trees. All the other boys had fled.

"Isaac," Alif said in alarm. "Where is Isaac?"

They searched with desperate haste and found Isaac on the edge of the track. A neat row of red holes had stitched his ragged shirt to his back. He was face down and his life blood had drained in a large red pool in which he lay. His rifle lay inches from his outstretched hand with its single bullet still unfired.

Daniel stared down in horror. Alif crouched beside Isaac and began to cry. He couldn't bring himself to touch Isaac's rifle.

The armoured car came back, hunting for the prey it had missed.

Daniel heard its snarl of power and grabbed at Alif's hand. He tried to drag Alif away but Alif slipped and sprawled forward. Daniel let him go and ducked back into the trees. He brought the rifle up to his aching shoulder and pulled it back hard as he had been taught. He fired his remaining two bullets with no effect.

The gunner inside the speeding Saladin failed to see him, instead he was concentrating on Alif who was still struggling to get off the track. The machine gun hammered fire and Alif was cut to pieces like human meat caught in an invisible mincing machine. Then the Saladin ran him down and ran over him.

Daniel dropped his useless rifle and backed away. He was numb with shock and did not dare to return to his friends. Only instinct was left as he turned and ran back through the palm trees. His shoulder was agony and tears streamed down his face.

Okwela was hunting for the front line, praying that he would find real soldiers to command. The boys were there to plug the gaps in the ranks and he had not yet grasped the awful fact that the ranks were shattered beyond repair, and that the men he had left behind at the front line had been overrun and were mostly dead. The Federal breakthrough was irreversible.

A Mig shrieked overhead but they were clear of its attack path and Okwela twisted in his seat to shake his revolver furiously at the deafening sky. Shells were carving up the plantation and corpses were sprawled around many of the craters. A few wounded men were crawling through the palms and Okwela saw abandoned weapons littered among the tangles of decapitated palm fronds. There were Lee Enfields, a few automatic rifles, and a Bren gun still set up on its tripod legs. He looked round for the unarmed boys who were supposed to arm themselves on the battlefield, but they were nowhere to be seen.

The jeep jolted out on to the main road again and the driver swung right towards Owerri.

"You are going the wrong way!" Okwela howled angrily and grabbed at the wheel. The jeep skidded towards the palms on the opposite side before his strength and authority won the battle and the wheel was wrenched round. The driver was sullen as he resumed control and the jeep raced south to eternity.

Okwela had been forced to drop his revolver as he wrestled for the wheel with one hand, and now he bent forward and groped for the weapon on the floor between his feet. His hand closed over the butt as the jeep turned a corner and then the driver yelled and braked hard. Okwela was thrown forward and banged his head on the steel bodywork. He struggled up and through a red film from his cut scalp he saw two Saladin armoured cars advancing down the road towards them.

The driver was spinning the wheel frantically, aiming for a gap in the trees on their left. Okwela saw the red muzzle flash from the leading car's 76 mm gun and a split second later the explosion heaved up the earth behind them. The jeep bucked high in the air as it left the road but came down on four wheels intact and shot through the screen of palms.

Miraculously they escaped a head-on collision with the tree trunks and emerged on to another dirt track that had been cleared through the plantation. Okwela breathed a sigh of relief a second too soon, for rushing toward them and blocking the new track was another Saladin. He realized they were everywhere, like a plague of steel locusts.

The driver was braking, searching desperately for another avenue of escape. Okwela knew it was hopeless and there was only one possible end. There was only one honourable way to die.

"Full speed!" he cried defiantly. "Ram the armoured car! Destroy it!"

His driver hesitated, but then stamped obediently on the accelerator. The jeep charged forward and for a second it seemed as though the crash was unavoidable. Then the Saladin's machine gun opened fire at point blank range and pumped a continuous stream of high velocity bullets into the jeep. The driver fell back from the wheel amid crimson fountains of his own blood and Okwela was flung to one side as the jeep went out of control. The jeep crashed into the palms and Okwela tumbled out.

He was dying slowly, the right side of his chest was smashed and a bullet hole had punched through his right thigh. There was no feeling, just a remote awareness that the revolver was still gripped in his right hand. He struggled to get up, cursing the useless left arm with its wrist still trapped neatly inside his tunic. Somehow he regained his feet and moved toward the armoured car. The vehicle had stopped but its outline was hazy. His feet refused to walk in a direct line and he weaved like a man drunk on the potent root beer which the women chewed and spat into bowls in the jungle villages.

The revolver had swollen in his hand, becoming unbelievably large and heavy so that he could not hold it level. The barrel pointed limply at the red dirt.

He thought suddenly of Victoria, of Matthew and Mark. They were no longer dead in Kano, they were waiting for him at the end of this road — with Jesus! He took another weakening step forward.

The Saladin's machine gun fired a casual burst and severed him at the waist.

* * *

After a moment the turret hatch of the Saladin was pushed open and David Katsina climbed out. He filled his lungs with fresh air, paused to listen to the sweet music of the continuing shell fire, and then dropped lazily to the ground. He needed to stretch his cramped legs, and enemy officers were entitled to the *coup de grace!* Already his smart battle tunic was specked with spots of blood, and as he approached Okwela he drew and cocked his revolver.

He put the gun to the back of Okwela's head and fired an unnecessary bullet. More blood and brains splattered over his tunic. He looked back to his radio operator and gunner who had emerged to stretch and observe and blew smoke from the revolver barrel with the exaggerated gesture of a movie cowboy.

"The only good Ibo is a dead Ibo," he told his crew with a beam of satisfaction. The two Yorubas grinned.

Keep Nigeria One was the war slogan postered in Lagos, but it would be Nigeria without the Ibos.

12

MARY KERRIGAN stepped carefully over the patients on the hospital verandah where the river of sick and wounded had now overflowed and walked to the garden in the shade of the church. Stubbornly, perhaps reassuringly, the bougainvillaeas and the hibiscus were again in bloom. Maxwell sat on the wooden bench seat that had been placed there in happier times and watched Aliya hopping slowly up and down on her crutches. Her share of the food which Prescott and O'Keefe had brought back from Uli had briefly revitalized her tiny spirit, and she was demonstrating how much ground she could cover with each hop.

Mary sat down beside Maxwell. He moved up to make room and she rested a tired head on his shoulder.

She found him easier to talk to than Prescott, or even O'Keefe, but for the moment there was no need for words. She needed a respite from the hospital, and a man's company to remind her that she was still a woman. Without haste or fear of rebuff Maxwell's arm moved around her shoulders.

"She's walking good," he said at last. He was looking at Aliya. "Maybe one day soon we can try her with an artificial leg. It's marvellous what can be done with artificial limbs."

Mary smiled faintly. "You're walking pretty good too, Hank. When I first saw you I didn't think you'd ever walk without a crutch, but I notice you've left them behind." She paused. "You and Aliya are the only successes I've had at Bumaru. All the rest we just accommodate until they die. We've been out of medicines and blood plasma for months."

"Don't give up now, it's nearly over." Maxwell squeezed her gently, feeling the thinness of her through the white coat. "The rumours say Ojukwu has taken to the bush — or bolted in his private plane to Gabon. And the other Biafran commanders are ready to negotiate a surrender. It's only a matter of time."

"Then you'll be able to get out." She looked at him uncertainly, with love-bruised eyes. "What then, Hank? Will you go back to America and start the new airline you planned?"

"I don't think so. Max-Air Services crashed, and Tucker Airlines never got off the ground. There may be enough cash in my Swiss account to buy a plane, but right now my conscience tells me I should donate it all to the Red Cross or the churches. Without them we wouldn't be alive." He paused there wryly. "But I suppose I won't. I'm not a saint. Maybe I'll give half."

"As long as you give something," Mary said. "I came out here to give a year of my life to Africa. It's a small gift compared with Sister Bernadette and Father O'Keefe who have given

279

all their lives — but it's something."

Aliya came up to them with curious eyes. Maxwell absently fondled the curly black head. Mary smiled.

Maxwell glanced into her face. "If you came with me," he said softly. "We could call it Kerrigan Airways. How does that sound?"

"Like a wild dream. You told me once it was Claire's good head for business that kept Max-Air Services flying — but I'm not another Claire."

"There'll never be another Claire," Maxwell said. "But there'll never be another Mary either."

There were more and more wounded and defeated soldiers finding their way to Bumaru, each one with a new tale of rout and disaster, and finally Daniel limped home late in the afternoon. He had walked the best part of thirty miles and his bare feet were raw and blistered. His belly was empty of everything but hunger pain and he was staggering with fatigue. When he saw the cross against the sky he did not know whether to feel relief or shame.

Rachel saw him first as he emerged from the bush and sped to meet him, crying his name. As she reached him he collapsed on to his knees and pitched forward, burying his face against the front of her skirt. He was a man and it was unmanly to weep, but again the bitter tears rolled down his cheeks. Rachel held him and soothed him until Sister Alice and Sister Bernadette arrived to help her lift him up. In between sobs he told them that Isaac and Alif were dead.

"It was my fault," he said wretchedly. "I took them away, but I could not bring them back."

"Hush, child." Sister Bernadette tried to comfort him. "They had minds of their own. Perhaps they would have gone of their own will in time."

"No." Daniel was certain. "They would not have gone without me. I was the leader."

"Find him some food and bathe

281

his feet," the Irish nun told Rachel and Sister Alice. "He is our prodigal son returned. Afterwards we will all go into the church and give thanks." She started to move aside but then hesitated. The worn lines deepened in the dry yellow skin of her face and her eyes blinked. "What is this?"

Her hand reached out gently, and Daniel looked down at his chest. He had thrown away the twist of grass around his arm which had marked him as a soldier, but he had forgotten the fetish amulet which still hung from his neck. Now the small leather bag on its loop of string lay in the open, uncertain hand of the nun.

"It is nothing!" Daniel said and he tore it away. The string cut deep into the back of his neck before it snapped and he hurled the fetish into the bush. This time he had no intention of retrieving it.

"There is no God for the Ibos," he told them in despair. "There is no Jesus. There is no Chuku. There is no power in a fetish. It is useless to pray! The Hausa and the Yoruba are coming and nothing can save us. They have killed everyone at Aba. They are killing everyone at Owerri. They will come here and kill everyone at Bumaru!"

"Give him some food," Sister Bernadette repeated gently. "Take good care of him."

★ ★ ★

During the night more soldiers pulled back into Bumaru, some of them wearing scraps of uniforms and a few still carrying their arms. With them were a couple of bewildered boy porters with two-foot long, Biafran-made rockets with tin fins balanced upon their heads. The crude launching frames which should have fired the rockets had been left far behind, but the porters steadfastly refused to abandon their now useless burdens.

O'Keefe groaned when he saw how

his flock had again swollen, for the food they had brought from Uli was disappearing fast. The news that Owerri had been evacuated meant the road to Uli was now wide open to Federal attack and they must expect supplies to be totally disrupted. Nothing would reach them now until the conquerors organized their own food distribution, and even if the intention was there the confusion of Biafra's demise could cause days or even weeks of delay.

There was also the uncomfortable fact that Bumaru lay between the advancing Federal forces at Owerri, and the Uli airstrip which they would have to neutralize to end the war. O'Keefe hoped that Daniel and all the others had exaggerated their lurid stories of Federal atrocities, and he had already decided to hold special prayer services throughout the day.

But first there was the morning food issue, and if he didn't include the new intake of soldiers with the carefully measured handfuls of cornmeal and bean powder they would probably use their weapons to take it from the other refugees. He sighed as he unlocked the food store and surveyed the little that was left. Then with Prescott and Maxwell to keep the queue in order he began to half-fill the outstretched hands.

In the hospital surgery Mary and Sister Ruth began to clean and dress the overnight crop of wounds. A small queue had formed at the door and each man waited in sad-eyed, uncomplaining silence, grateful that they had found somewhere to receive even the minimum of attention. Mary and the nun laid their first patient on the table, a man blinded by a near miss from a mortar shell, and carefully bathed the blood from his face. There was little they could do except bathe and bandage.

Rachel stood beside them, ready to perform any useful task. The oldest mission girl was now a full time surgery assistant, sterilizing instruments, cutting up sheets for bandages, and disposing of bowls of bloodied water. Her bright young presence was an asset and already it had been decided that when the war was over every effort would be made to send her to university to study medicine. Rachel was Bumaru's promise for tomorrow, one of the doctors of the future.

In the crowded hospital ward Sister Bernadette and Sister Alice were engaged in the task of feeding those who could not feed themselves. Some of the sick had mothers, sisters or wives to help care for them, but there were others who had lost all contact with their families. Sometimes Sister Bernadette thought she would like to see General Gowon and Colonel Ojukwu forced to work for just one day in this ward. She would like them to smell the stench of the horrors they had inflicted, to soil their hands literally with the blood and the faeces and the suppuration from the rotting wounds. It was an unholy thought for a nun, but perhaps it would open their blind eyes, or stir some feeling in their hearts of political stone.

There was no cloud. The mission buildings, the village and the refugees all baked in the pitiless white glare of the sun. The sky was an infinity of savage blue. In the compound before the church the Africans and the three white men all kept their eyes down, narrowed and shielded against the bright light. The food queue shuffled slowly to receive their driblet of charity. O'Keefe thought of the miracle of the loaves and fishes, but he could perform no miracles here.

Maxwell heard it first, a faint rumble in the heavens. He turned away from the food queue, one hand was still steadying the shoulder of the old woman he had been helping to stand upright, with the other he shielded his eyes. He squinted against the hot burnished void but saw nothing. The aircraft were in a direct line with the molten core of the sun. He squeezed his eyes shut and looked down. For a few seconds he was blind.

The refugees turned fearful eyes to the sky, the men using their hands as Maxwell had done, the women pulling forward the hoods of their shawls. Prescott and O'Keefe stopped serving. Panic fluttered through a hundred hearts.

"Do not be afraid!" O'Keefe shouted. He pointed to the thatched roof of the hospital where big red crosses had been painted on a white background. "The aeroplanes can see the sign of the red cross. They can see the cross above the church. They will not attack."

He had calmed them many times before, but this time a Mig 17 was coming down for a closer look. The refugees scattered with screams of terror and then Prescott heard Maxwell yelling a frantic warning. He spun round and saw what Maxwell had seen; a group of soldiers on the edge of the compound were pointing a machine gun up to the sky.

Maxwell was running with clumsy, stiff-legged strides. Prescott sprinted after him but he had more distance to cover. The machine gun opened fire as the Mig flashed overhead with a thunderous roar. Seconds later Maxwell shoulder-charged the group with the machine gun and they crashed down together in a startled, cursing heap. The biggest of the Africans, a sergeant due to his stamina and size, was struggling to hold on to the weapon. Maxwell slugged the big man on the jaw with a punch that skinned his knuckles. Then Prescott reached them and kicked the machine gun away.

They had acted too late. There were a dozen soldiers in the compound who had doggedly clung on to their weapons as they fled the battlefield, and with one instinct they followed the unthinking example. A ragged volley of rifle bullets echoed the automatic burst to spit in futile chorus at the passing Mig 17. The jet fighter was already out of range, but immediately its flight pattern became a sharp, graceful curve as it turned back.

The pilot had not failed to observe his hostile reception, perhaps he had even been able to distinguish the tatters of military uniform. Also Bumaru was no longer a safe and harmless haven far behind the battle lines, but a possible obstacle in the path of the last Federal thrust to Uli.

"He's going to attack!" Prescott bellowed with certainty.

"And he's not the only one!" Maxwell added with a sinking heart. While every other eye was concentrated upon the returning Mig his practised ears had picked out the note of heavier engines high in the sky. He recognized two Ilyushin jet bombers.

The Africans scattered like cattle struck by lightning. Shrieking women grabbed up their children or hunted round in hysterical circles. Cripples and babies were knocked sprawling in the rush and lay bleating like sacrificial goats. The whole compound became a vortex in reverse with people spewed out in all directions. A few individual rifles cracked for the second time, but most of the weapons were thrown away in the mad stampede for cover. Stark terror reigned as the Mig came down blazing fire, but above it all two urgent, conflicting voices made themselves heard.

"To the church!" O'Keefe cried with desperate faith, and with outstretched arms he shepherded a stumbling group at a run to the refuge of the cross. *"Everybody into the church!"*

"Stay away from the buildings!" Prescott warned with equal conviction. "Make for the bush!" He scooped up a fallen baby under each arm and steered another panic-stricken group away from the compound.

Rockets and machine gun fire lanced down from the Mig, chewing up flesh, bone, earth and buildings. The thunder of explosions almost drowned the screams of men, women and children toppling like ragged black reeds in the shock waves of erupting dirt, flame and flying shrapnel. The group who had fired the machine gun had fled in horror from the instant retaliation they had brought upon the whole mission. Only Maxwell was left, struggling upright with the weapon in his hands. The damage was done now and bitterly he emptied the remainder of the magazine as the Mig swept overhead.

When the smoke cleared and the dust settled there were a score of dead and wounded littering the compound. Maxwell lowered the machine gun and stared around. With casualties on either side it was hardly credible that he had escaped unscathed, but this time he had been lucky. He saw O'Keefe emerge from the church to collect a few stragglers, and then he remembered the bombers and looked up. The Ilyushins were great silver swords in the sun and they had dropped their bombs.

"Get back!" Maxwell yelled at O'Keefe, and then he heard a small voice crying his own name.

"Hankah, Hankah," the child's intonation was unmistakable.

He whirled and saw Aliya. The child was struggling towards him on her own crutches. Maxwell threw the gun away and ran to meet her, his stiff leg dragging and hurting abominably with every stride. He threw himself on top of her as the bombs crashed down.

The ground heaved as though split asunder by an earthquake and the air was torn by great thunderclaps of sound. One bomb exploded in the village, flattening two of the thatched huts and setting three others instantly to flames. The second bomb ripped out a deep crater in the bush, uprooting thorn trees and vegetation and blowing two Africans to bloody fragments. The third crashed close to the hospital, scooping another crater in the compound and demolishing the surgery wall. As the verandah collapsed and the surgery roof caved in the red tongues of fire licked along the thatched roof of the long hospital ward and began to hungrily devour the bright red crosses on the white circles.

The fourth bomb scored a direct hit on the church.

Thirty seconds passed before Maxwell pushed himself up on to his hands and knees. He crouched there in a daze with the vibrations still ringing in his ears. His shirt was shredded and he felt as though his back had been whipped. He became aware of Aliya lying motionless beneath him.

Prescott had thrown himself flat behind a screen of bushes as the bombs dropped. When it was over he picked himself up and looked round. The two babies he had hurled ahead of him to safety were bawling in terror, but there were Africans crouched close enough to attend to them. He hurried back to help Maxwell.

He got the American to his feet and lifted Aliya in his arms. The curly black head lolled limply like that of a golliwog doll.

"She's alive," Prescott said. He

couldn't determine exactly where the child was hurt.

Maxwell looked relieved, but then the dull crackle of burning snarled at their ears. He twisted round and saw the flames shooting up from the hospital.

"Sweet Jesus," he said in anguish. "Mary's in there!"

He lurched toward the blazing shambles of the surgery, ducking his head behind one arm to protect his face from the waves of radiant heat and smoke. Prescott thrust Aliya into the uncertain arms of the nearest African woman and plunged full tilt after the American.

They reached the surgery together, scrambling over the ruined timbers of the verandah and pushing through the flame-wreathed door frame which was now tilted at a crazy angle of forty-five degrees. They were choked and blinded by the poisonous smoke and the intense heat made them falter. The fire roared furiously and clumps of burning thatch rained down from the roof. Rachel sprawled unconscious beneath an overturned rack of forceps, scalpels and bowls, while Ruth Ekwensi lay crumpled on her back with her mouth open and her eyes fixed in the unmistakable glazed stare of death. A razor-edged sliver of shrapnel had sliced through the femoral artery in the nun's thigh and the bright red blood was still spurting. While Prescott stared down in horror the spurts lessoned and stopped.

"There," Maxwell croaked. His throat was raw and one word was all he could manage.

Prescott saw the white coat. A heavy roof timber had crashed down and pinned Mary to the operating table on top of her patient. The timber was burning and she was groaning feebly.

Maxwell stumbled towards her and made an effort to lift the timber. He was gasping and cursing but couldn't get the right leverage. Prescott moved round to the other side of the table and got his shoulder beneath the beam. A flame seared his cheek and singed his eyebrows. He strained upward and the timber moved. Maxwell dragged Mary free and she slumped to the floor. Prescott let the beam fall back. He was certain the African on the table was dead. He was coughing helplessly as he caught up with Maxwell and together they carried Mary out. She was an unconscious weight and there was blood all over the right shoulder and breast of her white coat.

★ ★ ★

Daniel had fallen into a deep exhausted sleep after his long walk back to Bumaru. He didn't wake until he heard the gunfire and then the terrifying thunder of the warplanes overhead. It was a living continuation of his personal nightmares and for the first few minutes he simply curled up into a petrified ball. When the explosions stopped he waited for another minute until he was sure that the planes had departed, then he got up slowly from his bed. His mouth was dry and he was shaking with limbs of jelly, but he peeped warily out of the long accommodation building to see what had happened.

The first thing he saw was the hospital wrapped in flames.

The next thing he saw was Prescott and Maxwell staggering clear with Mary Kerrigan. They laid her down gently and crouched over her with anxious, smoke-streaked faces.

A new fear suddenly knifed through Daniel's heart. Rachel always worked with the white nurse when she was in surgery. If Mary had been inside when the fire started then Rachel would have been with her. He couldn't see Rachel anywhere in the compound which meant that she must still be trapped by the flames.

The thought was a blind certainty and in the same second that it flashed through his mind Daniel leaped down from the verandah and began running.

298

Prescott looked up startled as the boy dashed past, but for the moment he was too spent to do more than watch. Daniel disappeared through the fiery doorway and agonizing moments passed before he emerged again. He was dragging Rachel out by the shoulders and a group of Africans hurried to help him.

The surgery end of the hospital was now a red-hearted furnace. There was no hope of getting back inside, but from the hospital ward the trapped patients were screaming for help. Sister Bernadette and Sister Alice were shocked and bruised but they were struggling to organize the evacuation of those who could be moved. Prescott left Maxwell to look after Mary and pushed himself up to lend a hand. Some of the less terrified Africans had poked their heads tentatively from the bush and he shouted to the able-bodied men to join him.

Rachel's eyes flickered and opened. She had been stunned by a blow to the head and her brain was dizzy, but after a moment it cleared. She realized what was happening and recognized Daniel crouched beside her.

"It's alright." Daniel's throat was blistered and choked with emotion. "I saved you."

Rachel smiled faintly. Her hand found his and squeezed gently. Then she heard Prescott appealing for help and rolled her head to one side.

"Daniel," her voice was weak. "There are still patients in the hospital. You must help to save them too."

Daniel hesitated. He was only in love with Rachel.

"Please," she begged him.

He swallowed painfully, then nodded and ran to obey.

★ ★ ★

Ten minutes later the whole length of the hospital roof collapsed, sending up great jets of flame and sparks, but by then they had dragged all

300

of the patients clear. Prescott stood back with Daniel at his side, both of them smoke-grimed and red-eyed, and smarting from their burns. There was no water available in sufficient quantity to douse the flames, so now they could only watch, as the luckless Africans in the village had already watched the bulk of their homes consumed to ashes.

Prescott was still not aware of the full extent of the tragedy that had overtaken Bumaru, and when Alice Idoma pulled at his sleeve he turned and stared at her blankly. Her dark face was filled with sorrow and her brown eyes filled with tears. She couldn't speak and after a moment of hesitation he allowed her to lead him towards the church. It was not until he glanced up to see the gaping hole in the roof and the broken cross that he realized the church had been hit.

Suddenly, like a hammer blow to the heart, he knew. He quickened his pace but in the same second he also knew that it was too late. He slowed to avoid treading on the heels of the nun and entered the church doorway behind her.

Miraculously the four walls of the church were still standing and there had been no fire, but the interior was a wrecked and splintered shambles. The altar and most of the bench seats had been reduced to kindling and the horrific bits and pieces of those who had crowded there for shelter were splashed everywhere.

One body was still recognizable, still mercifully intact inside the black robe. It lay in the doorway, the arms widespread in the sign of a fallen cross.

Sister Bernadette knelt beside him and gently stroked the white hair. Her eyes were wet and with her free hand she held her crucifix to her trembling lips.

Father Liam O'Keefe was dead.

13

THEY dug two graves in the small garden beside the church, in the shade of the bougainvillaeas, and there they laid O'Keefe and Ruth Ekwensi to rest. While the graves were being prepared Daniel fashioned two wooden crosses and carved their names and the date. Prescott searched inside the church and finally found the altar cross and the Bible. He wiped blood and blew dust from the latter and took them both to Sister Bernadette. She was already supervising the transformation of the accommodation building into a makeshift hospital, but she paused to receive the precious gifts. She pressed the cross to her cheek and the Bible to her breast, and for a few moments she closed her faded eyes. Tears squeezed from under her eyelids but when she spoke her voice, although low, was clear and steady.

"When we can get a priest we'll hold the requiem mass, but for now we'll hold a memorial service in the compound. Please find me a table for an altar, and a clean altar cloth — and the chalice!"

"Of course," Prescott said gently. He wanted to touch her but she was far beyond his reach. Her only comfort was her belief in God. He steeled himself to re-enter the church and search again.

"And the candlesticks, Geoffrey," she said as he left. "We must light the candles."

The service was the most moving Prescott had ever heard. Held under the scorching African sun, beside the still smouldering embers of the burned-out hospital, the prayers for the dead, for the sick and wounded, for Africa and for all mankind, all carried the firm reverence of utmost sincerity. Not once did Sister Bernadette's voice falter and although there were moist faces all around, her eyes were now dry of tears.

Sister Alice, Rachel and Daniel wept unashamed.

The Africans who had gathered in strength listened in hushed silence, a grieving, attentive congregation. Not a baby cried and the wounded held back their groans and whimpers. When the songs of praise were offered they were sung with a vast depth of feeling and the massed voices soared high into the blue acoustic dome of the heavens.

Prescott felt humbled, and knew that Liam O'Keefe had neither lived nor died in vain. He was part of something eternal which his own transitory spirit had briefly reinforced upon the earthly plane.

★ ★ ★

"We will rebuild the church," Sister Bernadette vowed when the ceremony was over. "The walls are still standing. We can build a new roof, a new altar and new seats. The cross will be raised again."

"Yes," Sister Alice affirmed. "The church, and then the hospital. We will restore the mission, and Bumaru will be as beautiful as before."

"It's a lot of work." Prescott looked at the ruins and found it hard to match their faith. "But Hank and I will help. For a start we'll move our things out of the guest bungalow and build ourselves a shelter. Now that you've given up your accommodation to the hospital beds you'll need somewhere to sleep." He turned to Maxwell. "Okay with you, Hank? Tomorrow we'll start on the church."

"I'm sorry, Geoff." Maxwell's lean face was grim but decided. "I'm not staying."

Prescott stared at him. "It'll be several days yet before you can get out."

"I'm leaving as soon as possible." Maxwell looked to Sister Bernadette. "Mary's hurt bad. She's gonna need a doctor, and proper medical attention if she's going to live — isn't that right?"

306

The nun frowned. "Mary had a large piece of jagged metal embedded beneath her collar bone. It's left a bad wound and the bone is chipped, and she's lost a dangerous amount of blood. What she needs is a transfusion, a saline drip, and antibiotics to prevent infection."

"But she can't get any of those things here, we haven't any, so the wound is almost certain to get infected. It's more than probable that she'll die!"

"If it is God's will."

"You've had other patients die with less serious injuries. She doesn't stand a chance."

"Mary is stronger than most of our African patients. Many of them come to us hours or days after they have received their wounds. And remember that we have had to feed ourselves regularly in order to continue our work. Mary is not totally deficient in protein and carbohydrates."

"If she stays here she's still going to die." Maxwell was convinced. "And what about Aliya?"

"She was concussed, and there must be some damage to the eardrum. She's still bewildered and doesn't seem to hear what we say to her."

"So she needs some specialist help, and the sooner the better. If we wait until things get back to normal it could be too late. She's only got one leg — she'll be deaf too!"

"God will decide," the nun maintained quietly. "We must trust to His Mercy."

"I don't mean no disrespect," Maxwell insisted. "But I figure God expects us to help ourselves." He turned back to Prescott. "Geoff, I want to take your Land Rover. I'm gonna take Mary and Aliya, and any other kids who need help bad, through the Federal lines. We can't wait for help to come to us."

"Think carefully," Prescott advised. "It'll be a rough trip. You'll shake Mary up and you could start her bleeding again. It might be best to stay here."

"No," Maxwell said flatly. "I watched

my wife die of cancer. There was nothing I could do to save her. There was nowhere I could take her where she might be saved. All I could do was to stand by, helpless and useless, and just watch while she died. Well, I can't do that again. I can't stand by and just watch while Mary dies! I'm gonna get her out of here — somewhere where there's a fully equipped hospital with drugs and medicines, where she can get real care and attention."

"I suppose for Mary the odds are about the same either way." Prescott didn't know whether to encourage or dissuade, but it was obvious the American had made up his mind. Nothing short of physical confrontation would stop him. Prescott finished doubtfully, "Which way will you go?"

"East." The decision was already made. "The main Federal thrusts are coming from north and south, and in the west there won't be a bridge standing across the Niger. I have to go east. I'll try to get across the border into Cameroon. Then I'll drive down to Douala. It's the principal southern city and seaport so there must be hospital facilities there. If not, at least it's got an international airport. If necessary I'll fly her out to the States."

"You'll be safe enough in Cameroon," Prescott agreed. "But you've got a hundred-and-fifty miles of hostile territory between here and the border; most of it virtually trackless rain forest, split up by swamps and rivers and crawling with Federal troops. It won't be easy."

"The understatement of the year!" Maxwell forced a glint of his old smile. "But I'm going to try."

He turned again to Sister Bernadette. "You could come with me. You can take care of Mary if she does start bleeding. In any case the Federal troops will almost certainly pay this place a visit as they move up to occupy Uli. It may not be safe here for any white woman."

"Thank you, Mister Maxwell." The nun spoke softly and without hesitation. "It is kind of you to consider my safety, but I must remain here at Bumaru. Until the church can send us another priest the mission is my responsibility, but even then I shall choose to remain."

Maxwell was silent. He understood.

"We shall pray for you," Sister Bernadette assured him.

"Thank you." Maxwell knew it was her seal of approval. "Geoff, how about you? Are you coming?"

"No." Prescott's hesitation was momentary and then he declined firmly. "Maybe you're right and one of us should try to get Mary and the kids out of Biafra, but at the same time one of us has got to stay here. I can't leave Sister Bernadette alone. Now that O'Keefe has gone, I'm going to be needed here more than ever before."

"Then I'll go alone." Maxwell was still determined.

"You won't make it, Hank." Prescott

spoke with regret. "Not alone, and definitely not in my Land Rover. The moment a Federal soldier spots your white face you'll be taken for an escaping mercenary and shot on sight. If you go you'll have to try it with the mission truck — and you haven't a hope in hell without an African driver."

Maxwell wanted to argue but Prescott was talking cold sense. Maxwell glared at the Englishman angrily and wished that he hadn't pointed out what was obvious. His mouth tightened and he scratched through the soot-streaked straw of his hair with frustration.

Daniel and Rachel stood nearby, listening and reluctant to move away after the memorial service had ended. Daniel was certain that the Federal monsters would come to Bumaru and butcher any Ibo male who looked as though he might have been a Biafran soldier, and suddenly he saw a ray of hope. He pulled Rachel forward and spoke up quickly.

"We will go with you, Rachel and I.

I can drive the truck, and Rachel will look after Miss Mary."

Maxwell grinned with relief. "Now that really is an offer I can't refuse."

Daniel smiled. He turned gleefully to Rachel and was surprised to see her face showing less enthusiasm. She looked very serious and his smile faltered.

"Yes, Daniel," she said at last. "I think you must go and help Mister Maxwell. But I cannot come with you. If you drive the truck then Mister Maxwell can keep watch over Miss Mary. My place is here. There is so much work in the hospital that Sister Bernadette and Sister Alice will need my help."

"But you can come with me." Daniel's face was distressed. He would not have volunteered if he had not seen an escape route they could take together.

"I know." Already Rachel could feel the pain of separation in her heart, but she had borne it once and she could bear it again. "If I stay behind there will be a place for another child who will die without proper treatment. And I can do more here than I could do in Douala."

She paused and gripped his hand. "You *must* go, Daniel — but please, come back to Bumaru."

Daniel could feel more tears behind his eyes. It seemed that for the past few days he had done nothing but weep.

"I will come back," he promised, "As soon as I can."

★ ★ ★

Maxwell was in no mood to delay so the truck was immediately made ready. Daniel checked the battery, oil, radiator and tyres, and siphoned out the few remaining gallons of petrol in the Land Rover to top up the truck's tank. Finally Mary Kerrigan was carefully carried out and made comfortable on board, with spare blankets packed all around her. She was still unconscious and her face was pale and bloodless.

Aliya was laid beside her and there was room for eight more of the critically ill children who had been maimed in the air attack.

While Daniel and Rachel said their goodbyes and Sister Bernadette made a last anxious check on the well-being of her patients, Prescott and Maxwell stood to one side. Prescott offered the American a leather case filled with maps and they unfolded the relevant sheet over the bonnet.

"There's a good road from Enugu to the border," Prescott pointed out. "If you can get out of what's left of Biafra you might be able to strike north east and use it part of the way. There'll be roadblocks, but Daniel might be able to talk his way through if you stay hidden." He paused. "You're going to need a hell of a lot of luck."

"Then we'll pray for luck," Maxwell said. He was wearing his Colt 0.45 automatic strapped to his right hip, but so far no one had passed comment. The gun might have been invisible.

"You'd better take a few old rice or flour sacks," Prescott suggested. "Something you can use to cover yourself if you're stopped. Let Daniel do all the driving until you're safe across the border."

"Okay." Maxwell stared at the map for another minute and then folded it up. He knew he was going to have to play it by ear anyway, making use of any local knowledge he could find and hunting for unmarked tracks. He slid the map into the leather case and tossed it through the window on to the driving seat. He made one last try to persuade Prescott.

"What you said about being shot as a mercenary — it could happen to you, Geoff. We both run the same risk, whether we stay put or try to get out. We're white men, and that makes us automatically suspect."

Prescott smiled wryly. "I've thought about it, but I'll still take my chances here. The Federals just might pass us by."

316

"On the other hand they might not."

"There's no guarantee that you'll get through."

Maxwell was baffled. "I don't understand you, Geoff. From what I hear you and O'Keefe were always arguing with each other before I arrived. The two of you could never agree on anything, from the Garden of Eden to the African soul. Yet now he's dead you want to take his place. It's crazy. You don't even profess to be a Christian!"

"A man doesn't have to be a professed Christian to do what's right — or even to believe in God," Prescott said slowly. "There's many a Moslem, Hindu or Jew who is equal in faith and good intent. In East Africa I had the opportunity to study them all, but I couldn't learn how to choose between them, and I can't believe that God would try."

He paused and stared towards the fresh graves beside the ruined shell of the church.

"Besides," he finished simply. "No

one could ever replace Father O'Keefe. Even I'm not presumptious enough for that."

Maxwell shrugged helplessly and then went to fetch the rice sacks. When he returned Sister Alice handed him two full leather water bottles and a packet of food wrapped in a clean cloth.

"There's rice and corned beef," she said. "Enough for three days."

"That's plenty. In three days we'll be in Douala."

He handed the bottles and the food to Daniel who was already in the driving seat, and then gripped the African nun's hand.

"Goodbye, Sister Alice."

"Goodbye." Her hand was still and her eyes were downcast. "I shall pray for you."

Maxwell nodded. He wasn't sure what to say. He shook hands with Rachel and then with Sister Bernadette.

"Take care of yourselves."

"God will take care of us all," Sister Bernadette assured him. "Even if we do not understand the wisdom of His ways."

"Sure." Maxwell was suddenly uncomfortable. He held out his hand again. "Goodbye, Geoff."

"Good luck." Prescott's grip was hard.

"That's corny."

"It's British and traditional."

The joke eased the strain of parting. They smiled and then Maxwell climbed into the back of the truck and settled beside Mary. Daniel looked back and waved, and then, biting his lip, he started the engine and shifted the truck into gear.

Prescott, Rachel and the two nuns stood and watched as the truck vanished from sight through the bush.

* * *

"I heard what Mister Maxwell said to you." Sister Bernadette confessed to Prescott when they were alone. "If the Federal soldiers come here they could mistake you for a mercenary, and you could be shot. Is it possible?"

"It's possible." It was Prescott's turn to be uncomfortable.

"Then we must prevent it. I can find you one of Liam's robes and a white collar. You can have his crucifix. We'll make you the priest of Bumaru."

"Thank you." Prescott was visibly moved. "But I don't think so. I couldn't pass myself off as a priest, and O'Keefe's robe would be far too big for me. Somehow it just wouldn't be right."

Sister Bernadette bowed her head. She was doubtful, but she had tried.

14

WHEN the truck inevitably bogged down Maxwell borrowed the machete which Daniel kept in the cab and chopped a four-inch thick branch from the nearest tree. By trimming the branch and cutting it off to a six-foot pole he shaped a stout lever. They had thought to provide themselves with short sections of broken planks that had once been seats in the wrecked church, and these they used as mud mats under the wheels. Daniel gunned the engine while Maxwell sweated to lever the truck forward.

It was a process they had to repeat with soul-destroying regularity.

They pushed the truck north east through the crushed and bleeding enclave that was still Biafra. Maxwell's main hope was that with the Biafran

321

military collapse the actual fighting would have stopped, and in the confusion of overlapping areas of Federal and Biafran control luck might steer them through. There were no Migs in the sky which was one blessing, and so far the first hopeful sign.

After the first few miles Maxwell decided to drive. Their progress was slow and it made sense to save Daniel until they reached the dangerous outer limits of Biafran territory. The roads and villages were still choked with refugees who had retreated until they collided with refugees retreating from the opposite direction. Then they had all sunk into the battered apathy of despair at the roadside, or on the road itself. Maxwell made frequent stops so that Daniel could ask questions, hopefully trying to establish some sort of picture of the situation ahead. Most of the answers were conflicting or vague. No one really knew what was happening. Many of them were blank with shock. All they knew was that they were victims of the most terrible catastrophe in African history.

The land itself was ravaged by war and nature, ripped and torn by shells and air attacks, burned by fire, whipped and hammered by the torrential rains, and then baked dry by the blistering sun. Fat, sleek and well-fed vultures circled lazily in the sky. Of all God's creatures only the carrion-eaters had profited from this war. They had gorged themselves on the endless banquet of death.

★ ★ ★

They reached the Imo River after three gruelling hours, and found a bridge of wooden struts and planks that had been smashed by rockets. The whole structure was leaning crazily to one side with a gaping, splinter-edged hole half way across. The river was thirty feet wide, swollen by the recent heavy rains, and rushed fast and deep in a rich, red-brown flood.

Maxwell stopped the truck and got down on to the road. His left leg was stiff and ached but that was something he was learning to ignore. He could imagine the Mig attack that had shot up the bridge and turned a wary eye skyward before he walked out slowly on to the sagging timbers. Daniel came to join him looking apprehensive. When they reached the middle the bridge creaked and swayed. A section of broken handrail slid into the river with a splash.

"This is no good." Daniel ventured gloomily. He rubbed the back of his woolly head as he stared down at the gurgling water that pushed and sucked noisily at the tilted wood piles. "We must find another way."

Maxwell wasn't so sure. If they turned back they would have to hunt north or south for an alternative route, and he had a positive feeling that either way they would run into heavy concentrations of Federal troops. On the other hand the road they had been following over the past few miles was nothing more than a crude track through thick jungle. It's deeply rutted surface was only just wide enough for the truck and it was obviously unsuitable for any bulk movement of troops or equipment.

The jagged edges of broken timber were discoloured, a sign that the damage was several days old. As yet no attempt had been made to repair the bridge, and Maxwell's instinct told him that if they could get across it would be worth the effort.

Right now instinct was the only guide he had.

"Maybe we can patch it up," he told Daniel. "There were a couple of wrecked shacks half a mile back. We might be able to cannibalize some timbers from those."

Daniel did not receive the idea with any enthusiasm. He looked down into the river and wondered how many crocodiles might be lurking along the river banks or under the surface. Then he shrugged and followed Maxwell back to the truck.

They checked over their patients. Mary was sweating but still unconscious. The hurt African children stared back with dark, frightened eyes. Maxwell wiped Mary's face and wetted all their lips from a water bottle. He stared down at Mary for a moment and felt a choking sensation in his throat. Claire had looked like this when she was asleep, motionless, ashen, half way to death. But, he told himself, it couldn't happen again. This time there was something he could do. This time he wouldn't let it happen.

He went back to the cab and climbed behind the wheel. Daniel was waiting for him. He reversed the truck with a lot of shunting and wheel-wrenching in the confined space and then drove back through the forest. It took only a few minutes to return to the wrecked huts by the roadside and there he reversed the truck again.

The biggest shack had once been a

native store. Now it was burned out, looted and abandoned. The door hung off its hinges. Inside there was smashed glass and a broken table. Outside a faded poster advertising *Star Lager* hung half peeled from the wall like a dead flag in the lifeless air. There was a low verandah and they used the machete to lever up the long nailed planks.

Maxwell felt like a thief. It occurred to him suddenly that with the war over the owner might eventually come back.

Six planks would be enough, he decided guiltily. They loaded the timber on to the truck and made the second trip to the river. When they stopped they sat in silence for a minute. To Maxwell's imagination the river swirled faster and the bridge looked more unstable than before. It appeared barely capable of supporting its own weight against the pressure of water, much less that of the truck. He sensed Daniel becoming equally faint-hearted beside him.

"Let's get on with it," he said, and got out before Daniel could argue.

They carried the newly scavenged planks to the centre of the bridge. There was enough foundation for the nearside wheels of the truck, but there was a six-foot gap to be spanned where the offside wheels would have to pass. The new planks were seven and eight foot long, which didn't leave anywhere near as much overlap as Maxwell would have liked. However, they had to serve. He laid them out in double thickness for extra safety and drove home the old nails with a hammer from the truck's tool-kit to ensure they would not slip. Daniel eyed the repair with a dubious and definitely woeful expression.

"We'll have to lift Mary and the kids out," Maxwell instructed. "And you'd better drive. You're a good few pounds lighter than I am and that might make all the difference."

Daniel gulped and rolled his eyes downward to look at the hungry river.

"Can you swim?" Maxwell was suddenly anxious.

Daniel nodded. "Yes," he admitted reluctantly. "I can swim."

"Well that's something." Maxwell forced a bleak smile. "Let's give it a go."

They went back to the truck and lifted the children out as gently as possible. With Aliya there were six boys and two girls. One boy had a bullet-shattered arm which only a surgeon could save. Another was blind, his head and eyes swathed in bandages. The oldest girl had a deep shrapnel wound in her groin and was barely alive. They were all infants, between two and five years, but when they were moved only the blind boy whimpered. In Biafra even the babies had learned to accept pain.

They lifted Mary by the blanket that was laid beneath her, struggling to keep it taut. She stirred and moaned but did not waken. There were more rivulets of sweat on her face and Maxwell wondered if she was breaking into a fever. There was nothing he could do if she was, and he comforted himself with the fact that he was sweating profusely himself. The sun was going down but the atmosphere was still steamier than a turkish bath.

Daniel started the truck and Maxwell backed on to the bridge and coaxed him forward. As the front wheels rolled tentatively on to the crude and ancient planking the whole tottering structure creaked and sagged. Maxwell felt a moment of grave doubt. Daniel eased his foot on the clutch and the truck stopped. The bridge stopped swaying. Everything was still. Only the river gurgled.

Maxwell backed on to the patched centre of the bridge. His arms were outstretched. His fingers beckoned.

Daniel wanted to refuse. He swallowed hard. For half a minute his cooperation was in the balance, and then he remembered the battlefield where Isaac and Alif had died, and he had run away. He decided that he would not run away again. Perhaps the bridge would collapse or be swept away, but he would not run away from this new danger. He gripped the wheel tightly and eased his foot off the clutch.

Maxwell watched the truck creep forward. The bridge rocked gently beneath his feet and the groaning of the strained timbers made him grit his teeth. The bridge leaned to one side, but all four wheels of the truck were now on the planking and the piles were taking the weight. Maxwell backed up again toward the far bank and gave Daniel a grin for encouragement.

"It's okay," he shouted. "You're doing fine."

Daniel was concentrating hard. The wheels rolled slowly up to the weakened centre.

"Easy," Maxwell checked him. "Left hand down a bit. Left hand down!"

Daniel was flustered. He pulled the wheel right, then left. He was trying to remember which was which.

"Steady," Maxwell said. "Hold her straight and you're okay. Just keep coming, nice and easy."

The offside front wheel climbed on to the newly laid planks and Maxwell crouched low to make sure they were not pushed forward. Nothing moved and the wheel was dead centre.

"Lovely," Maxwell breathed. He looked up at Daniel's tense, agonized face and forced another smile. "Just roll her over slowly. That's all there is to it."

Daniel drove forward an inch at a time. The planks bowed and the truck leaned over toward the river. Daniel looked down at the swirling waters and for a second he closed his eyes. He tried not to think about crocodiles or drowning. He opened his eyes again and Maxwell was still coaxing him on. He kept his gaze fixed on Maxwell's hands, willing himself to obey the beckoning fingers.

The bridge tilted and the truck started to slide toward the river.

Maxwell saw it going and his heart stopped. If the truck went over there was no hope for Mary, no more hope for Aliya and the children, and probably none for Daniel either. There was only one way to stop it and he sprinted forward and jumped.

He landed on the nearside running board and hooked his fingers under the edge of the cab window. In the same movement he threw his full weight backward, hanging at arm's length to counter-weight the tilt of the truck. For a few seconds nothing happened, and then the sliding motion stopped. Daniel had stamped on the clutch and brake and was staring at him as though paralyzed.

"Left hand down just a little bit," Maxwell said hoarsely. "Then keep her going."

Daniel prayed that this time he could remember his left from his right and turned the wheel. Maxwell nodded approval and he let his foot ride up on the clutch once more. Very gently he applied the accelerator and the truck moved again. The bridge trembled and Maxwell hung back and prayed in turn. He could no longer see where the wheels were rolling and there was nothing more he could do.

Daniel closed his eyes very firmly, and with his arms rigid before him drove the truck slowly off the bridge. He didn't open his eyes or relax until they were safely on the opposite bank.

* * *

They walked back for Mary and the children and carried each burden across to be replaced carefully in the back of the truck. Mary was not unduly heavy, and the children with their shrunken stick limbs weighed nothing at all. While Daniel soothed the fretting infants with a few gentle words in Ibo, Maxwell took a final walk on to the bridge with the machete. He figured it might help if nobody noticed that the bridge had been used and swiftly demolished his own repair work. With the machete he lifted up the nailed planks and toppled them into the river. They were carried out of sight in a matter of seconds.

Maxwell stood for a moment and reflected that so far their luck had held good. Now it was sunset and the dusk shadows were thickening in the forest. He had to decide whether to push on through the night or wait for dawn. The canvas sides of the truck were clearly printed with the words CATHOLIC MISSION STATIONS — BUMARU MISSION, and it was all a question of whether the wording or the cover of darkness would afford the best protection.

He still hadn't made up his mind when he turned back to the truck and saw the two pitifully thin Ibo boys who had materialized out of the bush at the roadside. They wore the universal rags and looked scared as rabbits, ready to bolt at any second. Maxwell stopped.

"Talk to them, Danny," he said softly.

Daniel emerged from the back of the truck, twisting his head from side to side. He saw the boys and approached them. They flinched back but the eldest held out a hand like a shrivelled claw. The urgent words that followed, the belly-rubbing and the desperate, outstretched hand were all familiar.

"They are hungry." Daniel said.

"Tell them we're sorry." There was nothing else Maxwell could say. "We've nothing to spare. Ask them if they know anything about the road ahead."

Daniel nodded and more words were exchanged. The refugee boys pointed up the dirt road and gabbled bitterly. Daniel turned back to Maxwell and his face was crushed, all hope was extinguished.

"They say their village is further up this road, and it is occupied by the Yoruba and Hausa soldiers. There are many of the soldiers with armoured cars and trucks. All the Ibo people have fled."

Maxwell felt as though his guts had been wrenched out. His instinct had been wrong and he had destroyed the bridge behind him. Even if they repaired it again he didn't think they could get back with the truck. The first crossing had brought them within a hairsbreadth of disaster.

The boys were still talking. Daniel translated in dejected tones.

"They say the enemy soldiers have only stopped for tonight. Tomorrow they will come down this road."

"Damn!" Maxwell swore. "What a Goddamned sonofabitch."

He stared at the bridge, trying to think. Perhaps if they could hide the truck until the Federals had moved past? It was an idea, but it would take time for the Federal sappers to make the bridge strong enough to take a continuing flow of traffic and time was against them. Every hour of delay stacked the odds higher against Mary and the kids reaching Douala alive. Also the Nigerians would be sure to guard the bridge after they had repaired it. The truck had to be moved now.

While Maxwell racked his aching brain Daniel continued his conversation with the two boys. Finally he turned again, doubtful and uncertain.

"Hank, they say the village is three miles up the road. On the south side there are cleared fields where they plant yams and cassava. They say there are footpaths and level ground where we may be able to drive the truck. They will guide us past the village — if we will give them food?"

Maxwell felt a flickering ray of hope. He stared at the two sad-eyed youngsters and wondered if he would be mad to trust them. They were starving and he could not blame them if they proved to be liars and thieves. As with the bridge he could only trust his instinct, and he decided slowly that he had no choice.

"Give them a mouthful of food now,"

he told Daniel. "And tell them there will be a handful of corned beef each when they get us past the village."

★ ★ ★

It was dark when they turned off the road after another two miles. Daniel was driving with one of the Ibo boys seated beside him. Maxwell got out with the oldest boy to examine the footpath leading into the fields. The path was well trod and solid enough to take the offside wheels, while to the left the earth was cultivated but not too soft.

"Try it slowly in bottom gear," Maxwell told Daniel.

The truck moved gingerly forward. The village boy walked ahead to show the way while Maxwell walked behind the nearside wheels with his makeshift lever. There was no starlight and suddenly Maxwell felt the first stinging wet blobs of rain hit his face. The black skies poured down and he cursed as he visualized the hoed fields turning swiftly to clinging red mud. Then he realized that the storm would muffle the low snarl of the truck's engine, which made the rain more of a friend than an enemy. Circling the village full of hostile troops was not going to be easy, but perhaps it was possible.

Within minutes Maxwell was drenched to the skin. The rain thundered on the canvas hood of the truck, rattled on the cab roof and splashed in the quickly-formed puddles. The truck growled on at a snail's pace through the roaring darkness, swaying, twisting and lurching as Daniel struggled to keep one set of wheels on the winding path. They did not dare to use headlights and their guide shouted warnings whenever they were in danger of losing the way, his hoarse, croaking voice audible for only an instant before it was drowned in the pitch-black night.

The nearside wheels were constantly

spinning and churning, throwing up great clods of red clay. Maxwell pushed and levered until it seemed as though his straining back and arms must break. Every muscle in his body ached and his heart thumped fiercely in his chest. Trying to breathe sucked the merciless rain into his gasping mouth and nostrils and he spat and swore as he pitted his own failing strength against the might of the elements, the grasping mud and the stubborn, grinding weight of the truck.

There were times when he had to use their primitive mud boards, and the Ibo boy had to come back and lend his few miserable pounds of stretched skin and bones to get the truck moving, but slowly they made progress. Inch by inch, foot by foot, yard by yard the truck crawled through the soaked fields. After an hour the vicious, driving rods of rain ceased as suddenly as they had begun to fall, but the grim trial of strength and will continued.

Maxwell lost count of the number

of times the truck stuck fast, and finally he lost track of time itself. The night and their blind ordeal were endless. The path led on through nowhere to nowhere and exhaustion drilled into the very core of his being. He stumbled and fell, picked himself up, pushed, levered, stumbled, pushed and fell again. He was a dumb puppet in a nightmare jerked by the savage strings of necessity. He no longer had the breath or strength to curse and the sequence of stumbling, pushing, levering and falling went on and on.

Starlight filtered through the black clouds but Maxwell was too spent to take any notice of his surroundings. Stunted casava bushes and the dim fronds of broken banana palms went by unseen except by the Ibo boy who led the way. Maxwell was sure they were lost and eventually the truck would grind itself down to a final stop where he would no longer have the reserves to move it. Then it would be all over and he would sleep until the Nigerians found them at dawn. He would be shot, but perhaps they would let Mary live.

The truck stopped. Maxwell leaned against it and sobbed. He needed a moment to get his breath. He heard voices and forced open his eyes. Daniel and the Ibo boy stood before him, both of them grinning in the gloom. The truck was no longer tilted into the soft mud, but standing level with all four wheels on hard dirt.

"The village is behind us," Daniel said. "He wants the food we promised for him and his brother."

Maxwell sank into a sitting heap on the road, he leaned his back against the mud-caked wheel and rested his hands on his knees. His head hung down and there was red mud plastered in his yellow hair.

"Give it to them," he said with relief. "Tell them we're grateful."

★ ★ ★

343

They rested for half an hour after the two village boys had disappeared behind the black curtains of bush. Then Maxwell decided it was time to attempt a few more miles. If they were fortunate enough to have slipped through the Federal net he wanted to be well clear of the front-line zone before dawn.

Daniel was tired and grumbled a little, but when he was reminded that the Hausas and Yorubas might still be close he needed less persuasion. He returned to his place at the wheel while Maxwell crawled into the back and concealed himself behind a screen of rice sacks and the sick children.

As the truck jolted into movement over the corrugated dirt road Maxwell realized that Mary was at last awake. Her eyes were puzzled.

"Hank," she said slowly, "What's happening?"

"We're leaving Biafra," he told her quietly. "The mission was bombed and you've been hurt."

344

He started to fill in the details and it was a minute before the first fact had fully registered on her dazed mind. Her face became agitated and she struggled to sit up.

"Hank, I can't leave. I'm needed at Bumaru. You have to take me back."

"Easy now." Maxwell pressed gently on her sound shoulder and she subsided with a gasp of pain. "It's all over," he insisted. "You're the one who needs help now. In any case we're through the Federal lines and it's too late to turn back."

"But the hospital — the children — Aliya?"

"Aliya is here, and eight other kids who need a surgeon bad. We have to go on for their sake."

Mary rolled her head, looking for confirmation. She saw Aliya sitting on Maxwell's hip. The child's eyes brightened and she reached out a tentative hand. Mary made the effort to grip the tiny pink and black fingers. She smiled, and then her nose wrinkled. Fear cast its black shadow over her face.

"Hank, that smell — is it me?"

"No," Maxwell said. "It's one of the kids. But I think we're gonna get you and the others to Douala in time. There'll be a good hospital at Douala, medicines and surgeons." He leaned over and kissed her. "Don't fret, sweetheart, we're gonna make it!"

* * *

Daniel kept the truck in third gear. He was afraid to use his headlights and possibly attract attention so it was impossible to go too fast. He peered into the darkness ahead with straining eyes and cast frequent nervous glances at the black forest unwinding on either side.

Maxwell had fallen asleep, claimed by fatigue, and Mary and the children had fallen silent. There was no longer the comforting murmur of voices from the back of the truck and in the cab

Daniel felt totally isolated. He was alone in a hostile world of menacing shadows and he began to wish that he had not been such a fool as to leave the familiar surroundings of Bumaru. The events of the past few hours had drained his morale and he was convinced that soon their luck would cease and this mad venture would end in disaster.

Light was beginning to penetrate through the trees when the disaster came. It was a roadblock made out of a bamboo pole and two oil drums, and when he saw it there was only just enough time to stamp on the brake and skid the truck to a stop. He might have crashed through the flimsy barrier, but in the same moment he saw the three Nigerian soldiers with FN automatic rifles already raised and pointed at the cab.

Maxwell was jerked awake. For a moment he was too dull-witted to grasp where he was or what was happening, but then he heard the sharp African voices. Daniel replied in a frightened mumble. Maxwell lifted himself on to one elbow. A rice sack rasped against his unshaven face as it fell away and then he remembered. He lay down again and froze to the floorboards. The dissenting voices continued. Daniel was putting up some form of argument. Maxwell sweated and without any conscious brain directive his right hand began to slide toward his hip and the holstered Colt 0.45.

There was movement at the back of the truck. Maxwell felt the iced serpent of fear uncoiling in his gut. He knew a black face was staring inside. He was tensed for the curt shout of alarm, the moment of discovery, the end! And then the blind boy began to whimper. For the first time Aliya started to cry.

There was no shout. A shoulder brushed the canvas side of the truck and then the third hostile voice rejoined the others by the cab. There was more argument, finality in the voices, and then the truck jolted into movement.

For a split second Maxwell thought that Daniel had talked his way through, but then he realized the truck was in reverse. Daniel had been turned back.

For half a mile the truck rolled backwards, until it was well out of sight and hearing of the roadblock. Then Daniel stopped again. He left the engine running and walked to the rear. When he looked up at Maxwell his face was pessimistic.

"The soldiers say I must go back to the village, and get a pass from the troop commander." His expression twisted into rage and he clenched his fists. "I hate them! I would like to kill them!"

Maxwell hauled himself forward and dropped down on to the road. He was weary but the short rest had slightly revived him. He pulled the Colt from his holster and checked it.

"Wait here," he counselled grimly. "Because I'll be damned if I'm turning back now."

Daniel stared dumbly at the gun.

"Give me about ten minutes," Maxwell added. "Then sneak back on foot. Come up when you hear me shout."

Daniel nodded. His eyes were still wide.

Maxwell grinned at him and then strode off toward the roadblock, keeping close to the nearside edge of the road where the bush grew thick and close. He could feel his own heartbeat again and his mouth was dry. He wished that he had stopped for a swallow of water but it was too late to turn back. The sun was climbing and it was already hot. A flock of finches twittered in the nearby trees and a large dragonfly hummed in the still air. A line of red ants crossed the road and he stepped over them carefully. After the first few hundred yards he slowed his pace and strained his ears. His eyes were narrowed and fixed dead ahead.

He heard the soldiers talking before he saw the roadblock. The fine hairs prickled on the back of his neck and cautiously he moved into the bush. He crouched low, taking each step with infinite care. He couldn't afford to hurry and he hardly dared to breathe. Silence meant hope. Noise meant death. If he snapped a stick or flushed a quail he was finished. Sweat began to trickle down his face and down his back. He felt dehydrated. He wondered how long he could go without salt before he got sick. Then he thought this was one hell of a time to worry about that!

Slowly he circled through the bush, sliding stealthy as a snake. Then he began to worry about snakes. Suppose he stepped on a mamba — or a Goddamned puff-adder! He had to take a grip on his nerves and worry about the only threat that mattered, the present reality, the roadblock.

When he saw the soldiers they were only twenty yards away. One man leaned against the nearest oil drum with his rifle slung casually over his shoulder. Two more were squatting nearby, face to face in murmured conversation. One of them was drawing in the dust with a short stick, a picture or a diagram to explain something to his friend. Their rifles leaned against the oil drum. Maxwell looked round carefully but three appeared to be the total number.

Maxwell eased closer. It was so damned easy he was sure something had to go wrong. His heartbeat was loud enough to wake up the dead in Lagos. He got within ten yards and then stepped out into the open, his legs braced apart, arms outstretched, and both hands levelling the big automatic.

"Don't move!" he roared, and was startled by the ferocity of his own voice.

The three Africans jumped and their heads snapped round. Their eyes popped and the man with the drawing stick fell over backwards with shock and surprise.

"Danny!" Maxwell shouted. He filled

his lungs again and bawled louder, *"DANNY!"*

He turned his head fractionally to the right to glance down the road where Daniel would appear, and from the corner of his eye saw a movement in the bushes behind him. Frantically he whirled and dropped to one knee.

The fourth soldier had straightened up from his place of concealment, still minus his trousers which were around his ankles, but stolidly aiming his rifle.

Maxwell fired and missed, fired again and saw the man blasted backwards. He turned again but his stiff leg was a handicap and he lost valuable seconds. His three captives were no longer paralyzed and were reaching for their weapons.

The man who had been leaning by the drum was bolting for cover and unslinging his rifle as he ran. Maxwell hadn't wanted a shoot-out but now it was kill or be killed. He took careful aim and squeezed the trigger of the big

Colt for the third time. The soldier's flight became a cartwheeling tangle of rifle barrel and flailing limbs before he hit the ground and lay still.

Maxwell made another scrambling turn, cursing his slow-dragging leg. He saw that one of the remaining soldiers had fled in terror. The other was kneeling with his rifle raised to his shoulder. Maxwell ducked sideways as the powerful FN automatic cracked sharply and the bullet creased the side of his head in a tremendous thunderbolt of blackness. As he fell he did not know that in the last split second he had triggered off one final slug from the Colt and the soldier was also falling and dying.

★ ★ ★

Daniel was approaching at a loping run. He stopped short at the sudden outburst of gunfire but before he could decide whether to press on or retreat it was over. The fourth Federal soldier ran blindly into him and almost by accident Daniel impaled the luckless wretch on his machete as they collided.

When at last he plucked up the courage to continue slowly forward he found that he stood alone beside the roadblock. Among the sprawled and silent combatants only Maxwell was alive.

15

K COMPANY of the Nigerian Third Marine Commando burst into Bumaru with all the subtlety of a jet-powered steel tornado at noon on the day after Maxwell and Daniel had departed. The sun was blazing directly overhead as two of the heavy Saracen armoured personnel carriers rumbled out of the bush road and snarled furiously into the compound. The refugees fled shrieking and inevitably there was one shrunken baby overlooked to wail and squirm like a black maggot in the clouds of churned-up dust. An Ibo soldier with more desperation than sanity turned to fire the last bullet from his rifle at the leading vehicle, and immediately its machine gun chopped him down.

Prescott stood in what had been O'Keefe's room at the end of the accommodation block nearest the church, which Sister Bernadette had decided was the room best fitted to serve as a temporary surgery. He was in the act of shifting a large wooden table to the centre of the room where it would be under the light with room to work on either side, and he stopped in mid-movement. The nun looked up from the task of packing away the last of O'Keefe's few personal possessions, mostly books, church magazines and letters. O'Keefe had not been much of a collector of material things.

For a moment Prescott listened to the cries of panic and the insolent thunder of engines. They were sounds he had expected but hoped to escape. Sister Bernadette had lost her calm composure and was staring at him as though his face might soon become a memory. A bundle of letters dropped from her fingers and she took up her crucifix. Prescott straightened slowly and turned to the open window, and then almost simultaneously they heard the crack of the rifle and the shattering blast from the machine gun.

Prescott moved to the door and Sister Bernadette scrambled hastily to bar his way.

"Please, Geoffrey," she begged him. "Don't go out there. There's nothing you can do. It's best if you stay hidden."

Prescott hesitated. "Someone has to talk to them — stop them! We can't just stand here while they shoot up our people."

"I'll go." She removed an embarrassed hand from his arm. "They won't hurt an old woman like me. They can see I'm a nun, a Sister of God. They'll know I can't harm them."

Prescott wavered, he didn't like to hide behind the skirts of a woman. There was no guarantee they would treat her with any respect and she could easily be swept aside. He at least was an officer and he knew how to handle men, the right note of authority might hold them until one of their own officers arrived.

"Stay here," she repeated with emphasis. "And keep away from the window."

"Someone is sure to tell them there's a white man at the mission," Prescott said slowly. "We can't hope to keep it a secret. If I go out and talk to them they might listen. If they have to drag me out they won't."

"No one would betray you," the nun said. "Not after all that you've done for Bumaru."

* * *

While they talked Sister Alice had already moved out into the open to pick up the forgotten baby. She held the wriggling infant close to her breast and backed away from the six-wheeled steel monsters that had invaded the compound. Her heart was a wild, fearful thing that fluttered against her ribs, and she watched with wide eyes as the rear doors of the Saracens swung open and the dreaded enemy soldiers jumped into view. The commandos fanned out into a crouching circle with personal weapons at the ready. Those facing the lone African nun stared at her with shrewd lustful smiles.

Sister Alice sensed a movement at her side. A frantic grandmother had missed the baby and returned to snatch it away. As quickly as she had appeared the old woman was gone again, scurrying back into the bush. Without the baby Sister Alice felt vulnerable and defenceless.

The Yoruba soldiers had straightened up, showing confidence. There was no more resistance here and they began to walk boldly forward. But their weapons were still cocked.

"Please," Sister Alice said. "No shooting. This is a church mission — a hospital. There are only sick and starving people here."

"We want food," one man demanded. "Where is it?"

"There is no food here. We have

none for ourselves."

"You lie, you are fat and plump." White teeth flashed suddenly in the black face. The man had a scar over his left eye that had healed badly. He looked evil. "You nuns always feed yourselves," he accused. "I like plump women."

"Search the buildings," another man said. "They will have hidden their food."

But his comrades were no longer thinking of food. They were staring at Sister Alice. The man with the scar licked his thick lips.

"Come here," he ordered, and steered her to the corner of the building.

Sister Alice tried to slide away but suddenly the edge of the verandah was pressing hard against her buttocks. The soldier's grip was tight on her arm and she could not twist free. Panic filled her as she was pushed round to the end of the building, out of sight of the compound.

"You have nice fat arms," said the

soldier who held her.

"And plump legs," another observed. His rifle barrel lifted her skirts and pressed crudely between her legs.

"Plump all over," crooned a third. "So much better than most of these skinny Ibo girls. They are as sexy as dead chickens."

There was hoarse laughter, and then for Sister Alice panic became terror as their hands started to feel and squeeze at her flesh. She opened her mouth to scream as the scar-eyed man loomed close and then his thick lips were forced on to her own. They were pulling at her clothes and cruel fingers were clawing up between her thighs. She struggled desperately and then she was tumbled over. As she fell away from the unwanted kiss she was finally able to let loose a torrent of piercing screams.

While the others held her down the man with the scar was tugging open his belt, struggling to free the obscene bulge in the front of his trousers.

"I'm first," he bragged urgently. "I saw her first."

★ ★ ★

Prescott stopped arguing when he heard the screams. Instead he clamped both hands on Sister Bernadette's shoulders and swung her quickly out of his way. Within seconds he was through the door and racing down the long verandah. His first thought was that the screams came from Rachel but when he saw the wrestling group of men he recognized the black robe and white cowl of the nun beneath them. With a shout of anger he vaulted the end rail of the verandah and his right fist cracked out in a blow that sent the scar-eyed Yoruba flying bodily through the air.

Prescott clenched both fists into a double-handed club and smashed down at the nape of the nearest neck. The man collapsed on his face in the dirt. With all his strength Prescott lashed right and left and the soldiers fell back startled. They grabbed for their weapons and then Prescott stepped back smartly. He straightened himself with his head up and shoulders back, standing at ease. He didn't look down at the sobbing nun at his feet.

"Stop this!" he barked. "Stand to attention!" He stabbed a finger at the nearest man. "You — where is your officer?"

The man gaped at him. On either side black fingers hesitated on the triggers of their weapons. Prescott had hit the ring-leaders hard enough to put them temporarily out of action, and the rest were caught off balance. They stood undecided, hateful and angry, resentful that their fun had been spoiled, but waiting for a new lead.

Sister Bernadette hurried along the verandah, her face white with shock. She hoisted her skirts and clambered clumsily over the rail, for the first time in her life she was too distraught to go back and use the steps. She dropped to the ground and stumbled forward.

"Sister Alice," she wept. "My poor Sister Alice."

The soldiers were silent as she helped the African nun to stand. For a moment the scene fascinated them. Then their hostile gaze turned back to Prescott. More soldiers had gathered in a threatening half circle. The entire advance party had realized that something interesting was happening. The circle broke and Lieutenant Agama walked slowly through the ranks. His face showed surprise and he kept a firm grip on the sub-machine gun which was slung by a strap on his right shoulder.

"Aha!" Prescott smiled, hoping that he wasn't making his relief too obvious. "Good morning, Lieutenant. I hope you speak English."

Agama nodded slowly.

"Then I regret to inform you that your men were trying to rape this woman. Soldiers must act with discipline, Lieutenant, and if they forget in the moment of victory then it is your duty as an officer to restrain them."

"We have fought a hard war," Agama defended his men. "They have won many battles and many of their comrades have died. They have not seen their wives for many months — and the girl was probably willing. Ibo girls have no morals."

"She is a Christian nun," Prescott declared curtly. "Not a village tart!"

Agama took off his helmet and scratched his tight black curls. In his opinion the Ibos were only vermin and surely his men were entitled to the spoils of war after all they had endured. On the other hand, who was this strange and unexpected Englishman? A priest perhaps, but he did not look like a priest. Perhaps it would be prudent to tread softly until he knew.

Prescott could read the doubts in the lieutenant's mind. Now was the moment to press his advantage and suggest politely that they search the mission to ensure that there was no danger and no undue hoarding of food. Then perhaps they would leave. He searched his mind for the most tactful phrases, but suddenly it was too late.

There was a noisy clatter of rotor blades overhead. A helicopter appeared and made one lazy circuit around the mission before landing in the compound.

★ ★ ★

David Katsina no longer led his troops from an armoured car. Now that the war was virtually over and there would be no more set battles he preferred to make his inspections the easy way. Also to be chauffeur-driven in a helicopter was more befitting his newly confirmed rank of lieutenant colonel.

He had approached Bumaru in a contemplative mood. His reputation as a military leader was already legend, and when he eventually returned to Lagos he fully anticipated a hero's welcome. He dreamed of Lagos and the future with much satisfaction. He could foresee that successive governments must fail and fall as they struggled with the massive problems of reconstruction which now faced Nigeria. Gowon was doomed as surely as Ojukwu, and so were their heirs, but beyond that there would be golden opportunities. The political crown would wait for the war hero who had earned it.

As the helicopter landed his thoughts were interrupted and his attention was caught by the uncertain drama being enacted before the mission. He waited for the rotors to stop and then swung out a casual leg and stepped down. His neatly gloved hands straightened the polished peak of his cap and his tiger eyes narrowed. He put his dreams temporarily aside and walked forward. His commandos opened a respectfully wide channel and most of them grinned in welcome.

Katsina glanced once at his lieutenant and then stared at Prescott.

"Frenchman!" he spat.

"English," Prescott answered quietly.

"*Mercenary!*" Savagery, hatred and

bitter contempt all combined in the one word. Katsina's hand dropped to his hip and he drew his revolver.

"A historian, actually." Prescott kept his voice calm. "I was writing a book before the war started. It was rather stupid of me but I was too slow in trying to get out."

"Mercenary," Katsina repeated. "No one comes to Nigeria to write history, you came to earn blood money." He had enjoyed the war and profited by it. But he allowed himself a moment of righteous anger. "If it were not for the white mercenaries who led and trained the Biafran divisions then this war could have been ended in twenty weeks instead of twenty months. All of this bloodshed and killing could have been spared."

"Colonel, if you allow me to fetch my passport I can prove to you that I entered Nigeria legally before the war began."

Katsina was not listening. He did not want to listen. He had no time to judge, and he preferred the role of executioner. He lifted his revolver and pointed it at Prescott's heart.

"Mercenary — " He smiled his famous tiger smile. "Here is your blood money."

★ ★ ★

Daniel had been lucky. He had loaded the unconscious Maxwell into the back of the truck and then turned back, and although he had only vague ideas on how he would surmount the obstacles they had already passed the return journey proved to be incredibly easy. The village which they had been forced to by-pass during the night he found empty and deserted. The Federal soldiers had repaired the bridge at first light and moved on into Biafra. Daniel followed them across the bridge, but somewhere they had turned off to take a different route for he did not encounter them again.

Maxwell awoke with a blinding

headache when they were still a mile from Bumaru. He banged on the back of the cab until Daniel stopped and then climbed groggily down on to the road. Daniel came back to explain where they were and Maxwell listened bitterly. There was nothing to be gained by berating Daniel for what might have been, and with the petrol tank almost empty there was no immediate hope of making any second attempt. Maxwell climbed into the passenger seat in the cab and Daniel resumed his place at the wheel. They drove on in dejected silence until Maxwell heard the roar of the helicopter passing overhead.

He raised his slumped head slowly from his cupped hands and stared up. The helicopter was descending beyond the last barrier of trees which still separated them from Bumaru. When its engines stopped there was total silence, and he realized that Daniel had also stopped the truck. They stared at each other.

"We'll leave the truck here and

find out what's happening," Maxwell decided.

Daniel nodded and swallowed hard.

They got down from the cab and Maxwell eased his Colt from his holster where Daniel had returned it. He moved forward and wished that his head did not ache so abominably. Daniel followed a pace behind and they approached the mission with stealth and caution.

It took them a few minutes to ease their way through the final screens of trees and bush, and then through a curtain of branches they watched the scene in the compound. Maxwell's gaze flitted swiftly over the parked helicopter and the two armoured personnel carriers and he noted that they were all unguarded. The pilot and the two drivers had joined the score of commandos grouped around the end of the long accommodation building. Maxwell saw Sister Bernadette and Sister Alice pressed close against the verandah, and in the centre of the group of soldiers an officer confronting Prescott with a revolver.

For a few seconds Maxwell was undecided, but then he made up his mind. He signed to Daniel to stay back and then eased through the bushes until the nearest Saracen was in a direct line between himself and the group of soldiers. Then he broke cover and sprinted for the Saracen in a fast, low run.

He crouched behind one of the giant black rubber wheels, breathing hard. His head was splitting and he swayed dizzily with the pain. For a moment he felt that he was going to black out but then the moment passed. He gulped another breath and then hauled himself up on to the top of the squat, steel vehicle. The hatch to the commander's turret was open and he slid inside behind the 7.62 mm machine gun.

Through blurred eyes he saw the Federal officer bring up his revolver with the clear intention of shooting Prescott dead, and so he fired a deliberate burst from the machine gun over their heads.

★ ★ ★

Katsina twisted liked a striking snake, his startled eyes searching for the new threat, and Prescott seized his opportunity to attack from behind. His left hand clamped down on the revolver while his right arm locked firmly around Katsina's neck. All around them the commandos had instinctively dived flat or into a defensive crouch and Prescott hauled Katsina bodily back from his men.

"All you guys throw down your guns," Maxwell croaked hoarsely from the turret of the Saracen. "Chuck them into the centre of the compound."

"Hank." Prescott recognized the voice with amazement and disbelief.

"It's me, Geoff," Maxwell assured him. "See those guys do as they're told."

Prescott wrenched the revolver from

Katsina's hand and then let him go. Now it was his turn to point the weapon at the livid black face.

"Tell them." Prescott ordered.

Katsina screamed at him and made a belated effort to strike out with his fist. Prescott could have shot him but instead he blocked the blow and smashed him between the eyes with the butt of the revolver. Katsina fell with blood streaming down his face.

Prescott turned the revolver toward Agama to repeat his order, but the lieutenant had already cleared his submachine-gun from his shoulder. Agama's face was furious with no sign of reason or submission and this time Prescott had no choice. Agama's finger was already tightening on the trigger and Prescott shot him through the chest. The submachine-gun jerked up as the lieutenant was slammed backwards and half of its magazine sprayed harmlessly into the air.

The commandos were scattering in all directions. Agama's action had given them a lead but their attention was centred on the greater danger as they fired blindly at the Saracen. Prescott pushed the two nuns roughly under the verandah to leave a clear field and Maxwell fired another long raking burst from his machine gun. The soldiers went down like skittles in a bowling alley. Maxwell had no taste for the slaughter but with bullets ricocheting off the armoured plates of the Saracen he had to return the fire before one penetrated the vision slit and killed him.

Katsina lay stunned with blood in his eyes, but he was tough and his head was hard. He crawled forward to pick up Agama's submachine-gun, and then using the bodies of two of his men for cover he wriggled under the verandah of the long accommodation hut. The scalding rage inside him was almost as blinding as the blood from his wound and he blinked savagely as he looked round for the Englishman.

He saw Prescott crawling toward the

far end of the hut and shepherding the two nuns ahead of him. Cursing, he twisted his shoulders round and brought the submachine-gun to bear on its target.

Sister Alice glanced round and screamed.

Prescott rolled instinctively to the right. Katsina followed his movement with the submachine-gun and fired a burst. Great splinters were gouged in flying chunks from the floorboards above Prescott's head, and pain smashed through him as two bullets drilled his left arm. Katsina grinned viciously and wriggled closer. He thought Prescott was dead but Prescott's right hand was still closed around the revolver. Katsina got within five feet before Prescott opened his glazed eyes and shot him through the head. The bullet struck an inch to the left of the existing wound and not even Katsina's skull could take that kind of treatment. It disintegrated.

* * *

After the smoke and dust had cleared Maxwell climbed slowly out of the turret of the Saracen. Daniel ran to steady him and together they moved to help Sister Alice and Sister Bernadette as they struggled to ease Prescott out from beneath the verandah.

"Well, Geoff," he looked at Prescott's bloodied arm and spoke wryly. "I guess this time you have to come with me. There's not much you can do here with one wing. And after this little shindig your life won't be worth a bent nickel if you stay."

"How?" Prescott asked. "If you couldn't get through the first time — ?"

"This time we'll use the chopper." Maxwell grinned and pointed to the abandoned helicopter. "This baby is big enough to fly you, me, Mary and all the kids, all the way to Douala."

Prescott noted the stained bandages around Maxwell's head. Maxwell was sweat-stained and swaying and looked in worse shape then he felt himself.

"Are you sure, Hank?"

Maxwell nodded. He doubted if he was fit for anything else but he knew he could fly.

"Provided there's enough gas I can take us anywhere," he said confidently. "Danny, bring the truck up and start getting the kids on board."

Daniel was slow to respond. Rachel had peeped cautiously from her hiding place inside the improvised hospital and now she ran delighted into his arms. A minute passed before Daniel realized what had been asked of him, and then he grinned in embarrassment before grabbing her hand and taking her with him.

As they disappeared Maxwell turned back to Sister Bernadette.

"There's room for you too. After all this you certainly won't be safe."

The nun looked slowly around the compound. Four of Katsina's commandos were dead, a dozen wounded, the rest had fled. Her eyes were troubled by what she saw, but her voice was firm as she grasped her crucifix.

"Again I must thank you, Mister Maxwell, but again I must say no. There is still a great need at Bumaru."

"But you can't stay alone."

Sister Bernadette said nothing. It was Sister Alice who answered.

"She will not be alone. I shall be here — and Rachel, and Daniel."

"But when the soldiers return."

"You will be gone. We must take care of their wounded as well as our own people. If they have good officers they will not harm us."

Sister Bernadette smiled faintly at Maxwell's discomfiture. "We are all in God's hands," she said quietly, and it was her final word.

★ ★ ★

When the rotors whirled and the helicopter lifted up into the hot blue sky Maxwell flew in one final circuit around

Bumaru. The two nuns waved briefly, and then bent their backs to the task of tending the survivors from Katsina's commando. Rachel and Daniel waved for a moment longer before joining them at their work.

Maxwell straightened the helicopter and set a course for Cameroon. For a few moments they cruised in silence and then he glanced sideways at Mary. She smiled and her hand moved into his and gripped tightly. There was no need for words between them but Maxwell had to say something. He turned his head.

"Geoff," he ventured. "How do you feel about being best man at our wedding?"

THE END

A FOOT IN THE GRAVE
Bruce Marshall

About to be imprisoned and tortured in Buenos Aires, John Smith escapes, only to become involved in an aeroplane hijacking.

DEAD TROUBLE
Martin Carroll

Trespassing brought Jennifer Denning more than she bargained for. She was totally unprepared for the violence which was to lie in her path.

HOURS TO KILL
Ursula Curtiss

Margaret went to New Mexico to look after her sick sister's rented house and felt a sharp edge of fear when the absent landlady arrived.

STORM CENTRE
Douglas Clark

Detective Chief Superintendent Masters, temporarily lecturing in a police staff college, finds there's more to the job than a few weeks relaxation in a rural setting.

THE MANUSCRIPT MURDERS
Roy Harley Lewis

Antiquarian bookseller Matthew Coll, acquires a rare 16th century manuscript. But when the Dutch professor who had discovered the journal is murdered, Coll begins to doubt its authenticity.

SHARENDEL
Margaret Carr

Ruth didn't want all that money. And she didn't want Aunt Cass to die. But at Sharendel things looked different. She began to wonder if she had a split personality.

MUD IN HIS EYE
Gerald Hammond

The harbourmaster's body is found mangled beneath Major Smyle's yacht. What is the sinister significance of the illicit oysters?

THE SCAVENGERS
Bill Knox

Among the masses of struggling fish in the *Tecta*'s nets was a larger, darker, ominously motionless form . . . the body of a skin diver.

DEATH IN ARCADY
Stella Phillips

Detective Inspector Matthew Furnival works unofficially with the local police when a brutal murder takes place in a caravan camp.

BEGOTTEN MURDER
Martin Carroll

When Susan Phillips joined her aunt on a voyage of 12,000 miles from her home in Melbourne, she little knew their arrival would germinate the seeds of murder planted long ago.

WHO'S THE TARGET?
Margaret Carr

Three people whom Abby could identify as her parents' murderers wanted her dead, but she decided that maybe Jason could have been the target.

THE LOOSE SCREW
Gerald Hammond

After a motor smash, Beau Pepys and his cousin Jacqueline, her fiancé and dotty mother, suspect that someone had prearranged the death of their friend. But who, and why?

SANCTUARY ISLE
Bill Knox

Chief Detective Inspector Colin Thane and Detective Inspector Phil Moss are sent to a bird sanctuary off the coast of Argyll to investigate the murder of the warden.

THE SNOW ON THE BEN
Ian Stuart

Although on holiday in the Highlands, Chief Inspector Hamish MacLeod begins an investigation when a pistol shot shatters the quiet of his solitary morning walk.

HARD CONTRACT
Basil Copper

Private detective Mike Farraday is hired to obtain settlement of a debt from Minsky. But Minsky is killed before Mike can get to him. A spate of murders follows.

CASE WITH THREE HUSBANDS
Margaret Erskine

Was it a ghost of one of Rose Bonner's late husbands that gave her old Aunt Agatha such a terrible shock and then murdered her in her bed?

THE END OF THE RUNNING
Alan Evans

Lang continued to push the men and children on and on. Behind them were the men who were hunting them down, waiting for the first signs of exhaustion before they pounced.

CARNABY AND THE HIJACKERS
Peter N. Walker

When Commander Pigeon assigns Detective Sergeant Carnaby-King to prevent a raid on a bullion-carrying passenger train, he knows that there are traitors in high positions.

MURDER TO BURN
Laurie Mantell

Sergeants Steven Arrow and Lance Brendon, of the New Zealand police force, come upon a woman's body in the water. When the dead woman is identified they begin to realise that they are investigating a complex fraud.

YOU CAN HELP ME
Maisie Birmingham

Whilst running the Citizens' Advice Bureau, Kate Weatherley is attacked with no apparent motive. Then the body of one of her clients is found in her room.

DAGGERS DRAWN
Margaret Carr

Stacey Manston was the kind of girl who could take most things in her stride, but three murders were something different . . .

THE DRACULA MURDERS
Philip Daniels

The Horror Ball was interrupted by a spectral figure who warned the merrymakers they were tampering with the unknown.

THE LADIES
OF LAMBTON GREEN
Liza Shepherd

Why did murdered Robin Colquhoun's picture pose such a threat to the ladies of Lambton Green?

CARNABY
AND THE GAOLBREAKERS
Peter N. Walker

Detective Sergeant James Aloysius Carnaby-King is sent to prison as bait. When he joins in an escape he is thrown headfirst into a vicious murder hunt.

THE DEATH OF ABBE DIDIER
Richard Grayson

Inspector Gautier of the Sûreté investigates three crimes which are strangely connected.

NIGHTMARE TIME
Hugh Pentecost

Have the missing major and his wife met with foul play somewhere in the Beaumont Hotel, or is their disappearance a carefully planned step in an act of treason?

BLOOD WILL OUT
Margaret Carr

Why was the manor house so oddly familiar to Elinor Howard? Who would have guessed that a Sunday School outing could lead to murder?

THE MONTMARTRE MURDERS
Richard Grayson

Inspector Gautier of Sûreté investigates the disappearance of artist Théo, the heir to a fortune.

GRIZZLY TRAIL
Gwen Moffat

Miss Pink, alone in the Rockies, helps in a search for missing hikers, solves two cruel murders and has the most terrifying experience of her life when she meets a grizzly bear!

BLINDMAN'S BLUFF
Margaret Carr

Kate Deverill had considered suicide. It was one way out — and preferable to being murdered.

TREAD WARILY AT MIDNIGHT
Margaret Carr

If Joanna Morse hadn't been so hasty she wouldn't have been involved in the accident.

TOO BEAUTIFUL TO DIE
Martin Carroll

There was a grave in the churchyard to prove Elizabeth Weston was dead. Alive, she presented a problem. Dead, she could be forgotten. Then, in the eighth year of her death she came back. She was beautiful, but she had to die.

IN COLD PURSUIT
Ursula Curtiss

In Mexico, Mary and her cousin Jenny each encounter strange men, but neither of them realises that one of these men is obsessed with revenge and murder. But which one?

LITTLE DROPS OF BLOOD
Bill Knox

It might have been just another unfortunate road accident but a few little drops of blood pointed to murder.

GOSSIP TO THE GRAVE
Jonathan Burke

Jenny Clark invented Simon Sherborne because her daily gossip column was getting dull. Then Simon appeared at a party — in the flesh! And Jenny finds herself involved in murder.

HARRIET FAREWELL
Margaret Erskine

Wealthy Theodore Buckler had planned a magnificent Guy Fawkes Day celebration. He hadn't planned on murder.